You'll never get enough of these cowboys!

Talented Harlequin Blaze author Debbie Rawlins keeps the cowboys coming with her popular miniseries

Made in Montana

The little town of Blackfoot Falls

isn't so sleepy anymore....

In fact, it seems everyone's staying up late!

Get your hands on a hot cowboy with

#789 Alone with You

(March 2014)

#801 Need You Now

(June 2014)

#812 Behind Closed Doors

(September 2014)

And remember,
the sexiest cowboys are Made in Montana!

Blaze®

Dear Reader,

Here we are, eight books into the Made in Montana series. I must confess, I'm surprised to still be here in Blackfoot Falls. When I started the series I assumed I'd write six books and that would be it. Then I would come up with another theme or setting, and maybe even concentrate on urban books for a while. Turns out I love Westerns, cowboys and Montana way too much. I can't seem to leave. And thanks to so many of you readers who share my enthusiasm, I get to stay in Big Sky Country a bit longer.

Some of you have met the heroine, Melanie Knowles, in book five, *No One Needs To Know.* She's the high school teacher, who also volunteers at Safe Haven Large Animal Sanctuary along with her students. She wasn't on the page much and it hadn't occurred to me to make her a future heroine. But a few months later I happened to read an article about the Wild Horse Training Program and I instantly thought of Melanie. She'd fight for such a cause, no matter how unpopular it might be among the townspeople who hold her up to higher standards than most. Sexy, enigmatic Lucas Sloan is also a hundred percent behind the program, but when he comes to town he throws Melanie so far off course she may never find her way back.

These two characters quickly became favorites of mine. I hope you enjoy them, too.

All my best,

Debbi Rawlins

Debbi Rawlins

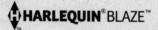

Need You Now

HARLEQUIN® BLAZE™

ISBN-13: 978-0-373-79805-6

NEED YOU NOW

This edition published by arrangement with Harlequin Books S.A.

For questions and comments about the quality of this book, please contact us at CustomerService@Harlequin.com.

HARLEQUIN®
www.Harlequin.com

Printed in U.S.A.

ABOUT THE AUTHOR

Debbi Rawlins grew up in the country with no fast-food drive-throughs or nearby neighbors, so one might think as a kid she'd be dazzled by the bright lights of the city, the allure of the unfamiliar. Not so. She loved Westerns in movies and books, and her first crush was on a cowboy—okay, he was an actor in the role of a cowboy, but she was only eleven, so it counts. It was in Houston, Texas, where she first started writing for Harlequin, and now, more than fifty books later, she has her own ranch...of sorts. Instead of horses, she has four dogs, five cats, a trio of goats and free-range cattle keeping her on her toes on a few acres in gorgeous rural Utah. And of course, the deer and elk are always welcome.

Books by Debbi Rawlins

HARLEQUIN BLAZE

455—ONCE AN OUTLAW****
467—ONCE A REBEL****
491—TEXAS HEAT
509—TEXAS BLAZE
528—LONE STAR LOVER****
603—SECOND TIME LUCKY^
609—DELICIOUS DO-OVER^
632—EXTRA INNINGS
701—BAREFOOT BLUE JEAN NIGHT‡
713—OWN THE NIGHT~
725—ON A SNOWY CHRISTMAS NIGHT‡
736—YOU'RE STILL THE ONE‡
744—NO ONE NEEDS TO KNOW‡
753—FROM THIS MOMENT ON‡
789—ALONE WITH YOU‡

****Stolen from Time
^Spring Break
‡Made in Montana

1

MELANIE KNOWLES ENTERED Safe Haven's cheery new office and sighed at the stack of papers sitting on the old desk. Well, no one said running a large-animal sanctuary would be easy. Though the next time someone asked for a volunteer, she'd at least stop and think for two seconds before jumping in with both feet. It would take half the evening to order more feed and cross-reference invoices, another three hours to grade her junior English class essays, and she still had to proofread her father's sermon before Sunday.

Oh, she doubted she'd find a single typo, much less a grammatical error, but her father insisted she have a look. Just as she'd done every week since her freshman year in college. That was ten years ago and so far she'd found only two misspelled words. No one could ever accuse him of not striving for perfection. He'd argue the point if she mentioned it. Not that she would. She'd always been a good girl, the perfect pastor's daughter. That was why she was living in the same small Montana town she'd grown up in and teaching at the same school she'd attended.

She made sure her jeans weren't too filthy, then sank into the new leather chair. So many changes had been made lately, all thanks to the generosity of the sanctuary's former director and her new husband. Annie and Tucker lived outside of Dallas but Annie still kept close tabs on Safe Haven. She probably felt guilty about leaving before her position had been filled. But Melanie honestly didn't mind temporarily sharing the responsibility with Shea, another volunteer, who also headed the board.

With all the new construction over the past few months, the job had been overwhelming at times. Thanks to funds from Tucker's charitable foundation, Safe Haven now had a new quarantine stable, a bigger barn, completely stocked medicine cabinets, a new irrigation system, equipment that actually worked and an almost-finished three-bedroom cabin for the next director. The list of improvements went on, but the bottom line was, so many more animals were being saved.

Someone knocked just before the door opened. One of her students hovered in the doorway. "Come on in, Susie." Melanie smiled at her. Susie stepped inside, her gaze sweeping the clean white walls and small galley kitchenette. "Wow, it's nice in here. You even have a window."

"What a difference, huh?" She'd opened the blinds earlier, giving her a view of the west corral, which held a pair of abandoned roan geldings that had arrived yesterday. In the distance she could see the Rockies. "They finished last week."

"Shoot. I wanted to help you paint."

"You can still help me put up the volunteer board and feeding schedule. Some posters would be nice, too, don't you think?"

Susie nodded, already distracted by the two roans outside. She reminded Melanie of herself at that age, smaller than anyone else in her junior class, quiet, a bit on the shy side, always eager to please. Another similarity was Susie's strong affection for animals. When Melanie had come up with the idea of having her students volunteer at Safe Haven, she hadn't been surprised that Susie's hand had shot up first.

The other kids had shown enthusiasm—whether to get out of the classroom or because they genuinely wanted to help was anyone's guess. But the project had progressed nicely to three afternoons a week and covered everything from lessons on money management to animal husbandry. Now the kids even received academic credits. Melanie had David Mills to thank for that. She just wished the new principal would stop asking her to coffee or lunch.

He always made a point of mentioning an upcoming school event or the program's progress, but his interest wasn't purely professional. Melanie may have led a sheltered life, but she wasn't stupid. And she'd never date her boss, even if she were attracted to him, which she wasn't. David was nice enough, probably too nice. At least for her. Wouldn't her father's congregation be shocked to know she secretly harbored a thing for bad boys?

Well, not crazy bad, just wild enough to bend the rules, someone who could kiss her senseless and not give a crap that her father was Pastor Ray. In high school she'd had huge crushes on two of the McAllister brothers. But guys like them had never given her a second look.

"Ms. Knowles?" Susie turned away from the window. "May I bring apples for the new roans? I hate seeing their ribs."

"They'll fill out soon. Doc Yardley thinks they're in fairly good shape." Melanie glanced at her wristwatch. "We have to leave in ten minutes. Have all the animals been watered?"

"I think so." Susie pushed the thick dark hair away from her face. "Are you coming back after you drop us off?"

"Probably." Getting to her feet, Melanie eyed the invoices, wondering if she should take them with her instead of making the thirty-minute round-trip later. Her gaze caught on the day planner she and Shea shared, and she groaned.

"What?" Susie moved closer. "Is something wrong?"

Melanie shook her head. "I forgot I have an appointment later." She massaged her left temple. Shea had agreed to meet with a representative from the Wild Horse Training Program. Unexpectedly, she'd had to fly to California for her job, so that left Melanie. "Susie, would you please make sure everyone is at the bus in five minutes?" she said, picking up the day planner and squinting at the name Shea had scribbled. The woman was brilliant when it came to computers but she had the worst handwriting.

"Sure, Ms. Knowles."

By the time Susie closed the door behind her, Melanie had decided the man's first name was Lucas. She gave up trying to decipher what came after that and set the planner aside. No doubt Shea had noted the meeting on the computer, but there was no time to boot up. Lucas could introduce himself. She patted her pocket, remembered she'd left the keys in the bus, glanced at the schedule board, then went outside. Kathy, a longtime volunteer, was coming out of the barn and pulling off her work gloves. She and her husband were the most dedicated of all the volunteers. They worked long and hard, and everyone had hoped they would take over from Annie, but Kathy wanted to move closer to her grandbabies.

"You taking the kids back to school now?" Kathy brought her hand up to shade her eyes. At 3:00 the September sun was still bright and warm.

Melanie nodded. "I'll be back by five."

"Levi's at the dentist but he's coming to help me dispense meds. No need for you to be here, too."

"Tell you the truth, I wouldn't mind getting home early for a change but I have to come back." She saw Brandon, the class troublemaker, threaten two girls with the hose spray, and she motioned for him to knock it off. "Shea made an appointment with someone from Prison Reform Now. It's an activist group out of Denver. They want to talk to us about fostering mustangs for the Wild Horse Training Program. Have you heard of it?"

"I think so." Kathy turned and saw Brandon still messing around. "That kid keeps annoying Nell, and he'll end up getting kicked in his behind. He sure rubs that mare the wrong way."

"Oh, well, that wouldn't be the worst thing to happen, now, would it?" She smiled, and Kathy laughed.

"You have an evil streak in you, Melanie Knowles, and I for one am glad for it. Lord knows these kids nowadays need a firm hand." She turned away from Brandon. "The Wild Horse Training Program… It's big in Wyoming and Nevada prison farms, isn't it? The inmates do the training."

"Yes, that's my understanding. Guess I should do some reading before I meet with him." She looked at her watch. Not much time for her to do anything but get the kids back to school, load her briefcase and take a quick shower. She hoped this Lucas knew there was no motel in town. The closest place for him to stay was Kalispell. "Come on, everyone. We have to go."

"I'll go chase out any loiterers in the stable," Kathy said, already charging in that direction. At sixty, she was small and wiry and didn't take guff from anyone.

Melanie should learn from her. One thing she sure could use was tips on how to say no. The bus doors were open, but only Susie sat inside, right behind the driver's seat, staring out the window at the roans. The image tugged at Melanie's heart. High school had been a lonely period in her own life. Friends she'd had in elementary school had decided it wasn't cool to hang out with the minister's daughter. Books and animals had been her escape.

Susie's face brightened when she saw Melanie board.

"I told everyone we had to go." She shrugged her narrow shoulders. "I hope they were listening."

"Well, they'd better have been or else they'll find themselves busy studying for an extra quiz."

The girl grinned and looked out the opposite window. A group coming from the stable was headed toward them.

"Everyone here?" Melanie asked once the kids had finished jockeying for seats. Despite the chorus of yeses, she did a quick head count in the rearview mirror as she started the engine.

Another recent improvement was the extended parking lot. Before the pad was paved, the gravel had scattered so thin the summer dust rose thick enough to choke the horses. She slowly reversed the small bus, swinging wide to the left. A loud pop startled her and she briefly lost control of the steering wheel. The bus lurched to the side, and she heard the kids' surprised yelps.

She tightened her grip on the wheel but the bus seemed to have a mind of its own. She scrambled for the brake and engaged it with all her strength. At the sickening clang of metal hitting metal, she jerked a look in the side mirror and saw the black truck she'd just hit. The bus had finally stopped, but her pounding heart nearly drowned out the kids' excited murmurs.

They all rushed to the back window, crawling over each other to see the damage.

"Please, everyone, be quiet and take your seats." Melanie hesitated before opening the door. She pretended to wait for the kids to obey but mostly she was trying to stop shaking. "Now," she said in a sterner voice, and they finally sat back down, still straining to watch the man slide out of the truck.

He was tall, wore his dark hair close-cropped, but he was far from clean-cut. At least three days' worth of stubble covered his jaw. Very calmly he walked around to the hood of his vehicle and assessed the damage.

Melanie sucked in a fortifying breath, then climbed out. She paused to stick her head back in the bus. "Everyone stay here. Understand?"

She got a few nods. Unfortunately, they came from the kids who didn't worry her. Dragging her clammy palms down the front of her jeans, she rounded the rear of the bus.

The man glanced up. He had blue eyes. Really blue. The kind of blue that made her forget what she was going to say. Then he smiled. She knew her mouth was open and she'd better think of something fast.

Rubbing a hand over his short hair, he turned to the bus's bumper. "Could've been worse."

"I'm so sorry," she murmured. "I don't know what happened."

"Right there." He gestured with his dimpled chin.

Her gaze followed his to the rear left tire. "Oh. A flat? I should've felt that before I even started the engine."

"No, it blew out while you were reversing." He glanced at the curious faces pressed against the back window. "Good thing you weren't on the highway," he said and crouched down for a better look, frowning at the other tire. "This happen often?"

"I don't think so, but I'm not the regular driver. I'm their teacher. I only use the bus three times a week to bring them here."

Squinting against the sun's glare, he gave her another look.

"Are you Melanie Knowles?"

"Yes." It didn't register at first, and then her insides did a little tap dance. "Are you from Prison Reform Now?"

"Lucas Sloan," he said, pushing up and offering his hand. "I'm early."

Thank goodness she had the presence of mind to wipe

her damp palms on her jeans again. His hand dwarfed hers, the skin rough and calloused like that of most of the men who worked the ranches in the area. But she couldn't recall a man's handshake ever sending a jolt of electricity up her arm. Had to be his eyes. Staring into them was dangerous. She'd lost track of the conversation.

She recovered quickly, and they both let go at the same time. "How's your truck?" She moved away to check his bumper. It wasn't as horrifying as she'd expected. "The school has insurance. Of course, we'll take care of it."

"I'm not worried. We'll let the insurance companies duke it out." He smiled, his teeth so white against his tanned face. "Let's focus on getting you back on the road with these kids. I assume you have a jack and spare."

"I hope so. We should." She paused for a moment, pretty sure she'd seen something of that nature behind the last row of seats. She turned to go have a look, then realized she was being rude. Melanie glanced over her shoulder to tell him that…

He was staring at her backside.

Her breath caught. Men didn't stare at her like that.

Again she lost track of what she was going to say. Swallowing, she tucked her unruly hair behind her ear and hurried onto the bus.

"Who is that, Ms. Knowles?" Chelsea was kneeling on the last seat to peer out the rear window. "He's hot."

Cody made a sound of disgust. "That guy's old enough to be your father."

"No, he isn't." Chelsea tossed her long hair and smiled at Lucas. Everyone knew Cody had a crush on her, including Chelsea.

"Excuse me, Chelsea. You'll have to move." Melanie could access the equipment without displacing the girl, but she doubted Lucas appreciated being ogled by a seventeen-year-old going on thirty. Or maybe not. What did she know about him? "One of you boys, help me pull this out, please."

Cody and another student jumped up. Cody was lean but strong and used to manual labor. Russ wasn't a weakling, though he was more the studious type.

Darn it. Great time for the husky football players to be at practice. She could've used them to change the tire. Now she'd have to call her boss to send someone. It would take forever.

She saw Lucas watching her, his brows raised in question. She gave him a nod, then asked the rest of the kids to stand aside so the boys could drag the tire and tools down the short aisle. Getting out of the way herself, she grabbed her phone off the driver's seat and left the bus.

"I think we have everything," she told Lucas. "It can't be much different than a car, right?" Her finger poised for speed dial, she stepped farther back so she wasn't blocking the door. "But if you notice we're missing something, I'd appreciate knowing before I call someone to come out."

He frowned, then turned his attention to the two boys wrestling the oversize tire and large metal box to the door. Without hesitation, Lucas hefted the box from the bus to the ground. It landed with a thud. Good grief—she'd had no idea it was that heavy.

Cody had some trouble getting the tire out, but she noted that Lucas seemed careful not to jump in and take over. He stood back, watching the boys work it out. While he was occupied, her gaze meandered down his lean body. His jeans were on the worn side but his white shirt was spotless, the sleeves deftly rolled back to the middle of his muscled forearms. Someone had taken care to iron that shirt. A wife perhaps? His ring finger was bare but that didn't necessarily mean anything.

Once the tire hit the ground, Lucas put his booted foot out to stop it from bouncing.

"Think you guys can give me a hand swapping out the tires?" he asked the boys.

"Sure," Cody said with a shrug as if it were no big deal.

Russ pushed his glasses back in place and nodded, not looking quite as confident.

Melanie shook her head. "I'm calling the school to send someone…."

"No need," Lucas said, unfastening the buttons on his shirt.

Melanie's gaze went to the wedge of chest he'd exposed. By the time she could speak, he'd undone two more. "No, really, we're close enough to town, Mr. Sloan. It won't take someone long to—"

"It's Lucas." He shrugged out of the shirt. "Would you mind?" he asked, holding it out to her.

"Of course not." She checked her hand to make sure it was clean but also to redirect her attention. Staring stupidly at his muscled chest wouldn't do.

After handing off the shirt, he took the spare and rolled it to the rear of the bus. His back and shoulder muscles were equally well developed, and if not for the three senior girls fogging the bus's windows, Melanie might not have caught herself staring a bit too intently. She motioned for them to go back to their seats, but they took her hand gesture as a cue to rush to the door.

"No." She met them before Chelsea left the bottom step. "Stay inside. The guys don't need an audience."

Leaving the tire with Cody, Lucas approached her, a faint smile touching the corners of his mouth. "They all need to get off so we can jack up the bus."

"Oh, right. I knew that." She watched him pick up the box of tools and head to the back of the bus.

The girls came spilling out. Mia and Chelsea had both applied peach-tinted lip gloss. "Oh, for goodness' sakes,"

Melanie muttered. Lucas looked to be in his early thirties. Teenage girls these days had no shame and few boundaries.

As if it had a will of its own, her gaze went to Lucas's bulging biceps. Apparently, neither did their teacher.

"Want me to hold that for him?"

Melanie blinked at Chelsea. She meant his shirt. "No, I'm putting it out of harm's way. You girls stay back. Leave Mr. Sloan some breathing room."

"He said we could call him Lucas," Chelsea said with a cheeky grin.

"No, he told *me* to call him Lucas. You may call him Mr. Sloan." Melanie realized she was crushing his shirt collar and hurried onto the bus to find a safe place to hang the garment.

Brandon was still in his seat texting. Mark sat behind him, one with his smartphone.

"Come on, guys. Get off now." She draped the shirt over the steering wheel, then followed the boys out.

"She really is a cool teacher. Our favorite."

Melanie heard Chelsea's voice coming from behind the bus. She paused and smiled. Though she wasn't bucking for teacher of the year, it was nice to know what the students thought of her.

"Even if she is old-fashioned," Chelsea said just as Melanie was about to join them.

The awful term stopped her cold. She almost turned around and headed for the office. The girl didn't know she was there. But Lucas did. From his crouched position, his gaze swept up to briefly meet hers. Melanie managed to find a smile for him but it was too late. He'd already shifted his attention back to loosening the lug nuts.

Old-fashioned? That was how the students regarded her? Maybe she shouldn't be shocked… No, not shocked so much as hurt. Though why should she care? She was their teacher. But she was only twenty-seven, barely ten years older than most of them.

"I'm going to call the school and let them know why we're late," she said. "Lucas, we have some water and soda in the office. May I get you something?"

"No, thanks. I'm good." He gave her a smile that should've made her breath catch.

Instead, she sighed as it sank in that Chelsea was right. Melanie wasn't anything like the exciting and daring women she saw on television. And she certainly wasn't a woman a man like Lucas would look at twice.

2

LUCAS STOOD BACK and let Cody tighten the lug nuts on the spare tire. Fortunately, they'd been working in the shadow of the bus, but it was still warm. Earlier he'd asked one of the kids to find him a clean rag and he used it to blot his face before rubbing the grime from his hands.

Melanie had checked with him once and then disappeared into the office again. He thought about sending the ever-helpful Chelsea to get her, but he wanted to have a word with her in private.

"I want to talk to your teacher," he said to Cody. "You don't need me. You've got this."

"Yeah, no problem." He put a little more muscle into the job. Strictly for show. The kid had it bad for Chelsea and all she'd done was ignore him and flirt with Lucas.

Man, the girl scared the crap out of him. Since when were seventeen-year-old girls so damn bold? Lucky for him, he hadn't been around teenagers much. But he'd been one himself not *that* long ago, and getting dissed by a girl like Chelsea? It hurt.

He took his time, scoping out all the new construction. The barn hadn't been painted yet. Another structure was missing a wall but there were no workers in sight. Could be the sanctuary had run out of money. That sort of thing happened too often. He ducked his head to see inside the older barn. Bales of hay were stacked in the corner. Several goats roamed freely, pilfering scratch from clucking chickens.

What interested him most were the corrals and fenced pasture. He knew Safe Haven could handle over a hundred horses space-wise. As for feed and vet services, his organization would cover those costs. If he could convince Melanie Knowles and Shea Monroe to participate in the program.

The log-cabin-style office was obviously new. He scraped the bottom of his boots on the mat, then knocked on the door that matched the green roof.

"It's open," Melanie called out.

He stepped inside and waited for her to look up.

She lifted her head, her brown eyes widening. "Oh. Sorry, I thought you were one of the kids." She swept back flyaway strands of dark hair and quickly remade her ponytail. "Are you done?"

"Cody is finishing up."

"That was fast." She tapped the stack of papers she'd been working on into a neat pile and stood. "I can't tell you how much I appreciate your help." She blinked at his chest. "You're probably looking for your shirt. I put it in the bus."

The faint rosy blush that spread across her cheekbones reminded him of Chelsea's comment. He supposed most kids considered their teachers old and stodgy. But Melanie? In that close-fitting red T-shirt and jeans, she looked barely older than her students.

Not until she cleared her throat did he realize he'd been staring. She came around the desk and went to a dorm-size refrigerator in the corner. She bent over and rifled around inside. Luckily, he'd stopped noticing how the soft denim molded her ass a second before she turned around and passed him a bottle of water.

"There's a sink in the barn where you can clean up if you like," she said and went to step past him.

He moved to accommodate her but got in the way instead. "Sorry," he said and noticed she'd blushed again. Her arm had barely grazed his chest.

Clearly Melanie was shy. Maybe that was what Chelsea had meant by *old-fashioned.*

"Well, this is awkward," Melanie said, picking her phone up off the desk. "Here you've done all this work, and now I have to desert you."

"You have to get the kids back to school, right?" He unscrewed the cap and gulped down half the water.

"I do," she said in a distracted voice. "I'll be gone for about an hour."

"No problem." He wiped his mouth with the back of his arm and saw that she'd been watching him guzzle. It made him self-conscious. He wasn't used to being around too many people, certainly not women. And here he was shirtless. "If you don't mind, I'll just hang around and wait."

"Oh, sure. A volunteer is in the quarantine stable. Her name's Kathy. Her husband, Levi, will be along soon to help. They're practically permanent fixtures here." She smiled and opened the door for him.

Lucas hesitated. "Look, what happened with that tire could've been avoided. Whoever's in charge of the bus was negligent."

Her lips parted with a soft gasp. "I hope you don't think I'm making light of the accident. I feel awful about it. In fact, I'll take your information with me and call the insurance company so they can get to work on fixing your vehicle."

"I don't give a damn about the truck." He hadn't meant

to sound gruff or make her flinch. "I'm thinking about you and the kids."

She looked away. "It's as much my fault as anyone else's since I drive the bus, too. I should've checked."

"Would you know what to look for?"

She frowned at him, her chin lifting defensively. "No, but I will from now on."

He smiled. "I'll show you if you like."

Melanie nodded, but he could see in her face she was still offended. Or feeling guilty.

Hell, he should've kept his mouth shut. He'd meant to help and it had gone sideways. When was he gonna get it? How big a price did he have to pay before he finally learned to mind his own business?

MELANIE PARKED HER compact Ford close to the gravel path leading to the office and resisted the urge to check her hair in the rearview mirror. Already she regretted using a little blush and tinted lip balm. Kathy would probably notice and start getting stupid ideas. She was always pushing Melanie to date or at least get out and do things that weren't church related. She knew Kathy meant well, but having a social life wasn't that simple.

It was 5:35. Melanie wasn't sorry that she'd taken an extra ten minutes to shower, especially when she noticed Levi's truck parked close to the old barn, loaded with supplies. Lucas's truck hadn't been moved. Apparently he'd felt no need to get as far away from the crazy bus driver as possible. She still couldn't believe she'd hit him. Usually there weren't more than two cars in the lot.

She scanned the corrals, pleased to see the geldings playing a little. Already they were getting stronger. Somebody had taken a bay mare to the second corral. The rest of the sixty-two horses Safe Haven had given refuge to were either in the stables or grazing in the north pasture.

No sign of any humans. She opened her door and heard laughter coming from the old barn. Kathy and Levi, of course, and Lucas. He had a deep voice, so she'd expected his laugh would have that low sexy timbre, as well. The sound even matched his buff body and rugged good looks.

She stopped halfway to the barn. Thinking of him that way? Big mistake. She swiped her tongue over her lips, then used a finger to rub off the residual gloss. Taking an extra breath, she walked with purpose toward the voices.

Lucas had changed his shirt. He now wore a black T-shirt, the same jeans and cowboy boots from earlier and a grin that sent her pulse into overdrive. He didn't see her.... Neither did Kathy or Levi.... They were focused on something happening in the corner. Even standing with his legs spread, Lucas was taller than Levi, who Melanie knew was close to six feet. His arms were folded across his chest, his biceps straining the snug sleeves and wreaking further havoc on her nervous system.

They were all watching Pinocchio, a notoriously mischievous pygmy goat, so they didn't see her approach. It wasn't until she came up behind them that she saw what was so amusing. The determined Pinocchio was trying to mate with Selma, an unfazed older Nubian nearly twice his size. The poor little guy would never reach, but it wasn't for lack of trying.

Melanie wasn't sure what embarrassed her more... watching the animal giving it his all or being embarrassed over something so silly. If it had been only Kathy and Levi, no problem. She would've had a chuckle along with them. For a second she wondered if she could back out of the barn without anyone the wiser. The thought had barely flitted through her brain when Lucas saw her.

That smile of his. Heaven help her, it was really something. She smiled back, felt the heat in her face and knew there wasn't a thing she could do about the blush.

"That was fast," Lucas said, mercifully uncrossing his arms and relaxing them at his side.

Kathy and Levi turned to her, as well. The instant the older woman saw her, she tilted her head, her sympathetic expression confirming Melanie's fear. Her stupid cheeks were flaming. She wasn't even a redhead but a mousy brunette. It wasn't fair.

"If I had known you had entertainment, I wouldn't have rushed," she said breezily.

"I put the invoice from the hardware store on the desk," Kathy said, and Levi added, "Jorgensen mentioned he could wait until next month to be paid if need be."

"Thanks. I'll keep that in mind." She looked at Lucas and wondered again about his white shirt. Had she somehow soiled it? "I'm ready whenever you are."

"I was going to help Levi finish unloading his truck. Unless you're in a hurry...."

She lifted her gaze from his chest and met his eyes. "What happened to your other shirt?"

"He didn't know I was gonna put him to work," Levi said, grinning. "This young buck stored feed in half the time it takes me. What do you do to get arms and shoulders like that?"

"Levi." Kathy gave her husband a warning glare.

Lucas just smiled but he seemed a bit embarrassed himself. "You want help unloading that truck, or what?"

"Not if you've got business with Mel." Levi clapped him on the back. "Go on. I'll take care of it."

"Am I going to hold you up?" Lucas asked her. "You got a husband and kids waiting at home for their supper?"

"Me?" She let out a laugh. "No."

Curiosity flickered in his eyes. "It won't take long to finish unloading. Maybe fifteen minutes."

"I know Levi would appreciate the help." She glanced

at the truck. It would take more like half an hour, though she didn't care. "I've got things to do in the office."

Lucas pulled a pair of Safe Haven work gloves out of his back pocket and left to catch up with Levi.

Kathy moved closer and bumped Melanie's shoulder. "Now, that's a fine-looking man. He's not married, either."

"How do you know?"

"I asked."

Melanie laughed. "You didn't."

"Of course I did," she said, and they both watched Lucas swing onto the truck bed with ease and grace. "I knew you wouldn't, so I figured I'd step in and make sure he was up for grabs."

"For who? You?"

"If I were thirty years younger and single, you bet." Kathy nudged her again. "He's real polite, too. Offered to help Levi without being asked."

"Well, good for him."

"Don't use that tone with me, missy."

They'd both continued to stare at him. Melanie finally turned to Kathy. "I swear, if you tell me I'm not getting any younger, I'll..." She just sighed. How pathetic. After hearing her mother say it a thousand times, Melanie should really have had a witty retort.

Kathy gave her a quick hug. "I expect you get that enough. Promise me one thing, though. If he asks you to dinner, you go."

She groaned. "Where is this coming from? He's here on business. I only just met him myself, and anyway, he isn't interested in me." Melanie frowned at the self-satisfied gleam in the other woman's eye and gave her a long look. "Should I be worried about you putting in too many hours?"

Kathy snorted. "I raised three boys. Good luck trying to shake me off. Think I didn't hear him work in whether or not you were married? He's interested."

"You said it yourself—he's polite. He doesn't want to hold me up, that's all. But you think what you want." Melanie turned toward the office. "Just don't embarrass me."

"Oh, honey, you know I wouldn't do that."

"No, you're right." Something had been bothering Melanie. She'd tried to let it go, but it still nagged at her. At least she could count on an honest answer from Kathy. "Would you consider me old-fashioned?"

Her friend's eyebrows rose in surprise. "Not in the least. Why on earth would you ask such a thing?"

"One of my students said something...."

"Oh." Kathy flapped a hand. "Kids always think their teachers are older than dirt. Levi was barely forty when the Weaver boy asked if he was getting ready to retire. Course, Tim's not a boy anymore. He's got two young ones of his own. Back then he was a junior and Levi was his history teacher. My poor husband hadn't even sprouted his first gray hair yet, and goodness but he came home in a foul mood that day."

Melanie smiled. Levi had been her teacher, as well, and she knew Tim Weaver, despite his being four grades ahead of her. And here he already had two kids. She wasn't anxious to get married or start a family, but sometimes it bothered her that there were no prospective men in sight. The guys she'd dated in college had been fun at the time. Though living in a dorm two hundred miles from Blackfoot Falls had had a lot to do with the fun factor. Here she couldn't sneeze without someone handing her a tissue.

"I guess I should get to work on those invoices," she said. "You and Levi don't stay too late, huh? Nina and her boyfriend offered to pull the night shift."

Kathy looked as if she was dying to say something but only nodded and headed out the back. Melanie turned and started to walk toward the office. She had a good idea what was on the woman's mind. Kathy didn't like Nina's boyfriend. He'd been a drifter who'd hired on at the Circle K. Sure, he was young and cocky, but he was fond of animals—otherwise Melanie wouldn't allow him to volunteer.

That was the trouble with living in a small town. Everyone had an opinion about everything that went on. Her being a teacher and the minister's daughter—it was a triple whammy.

Since coming home, she'd gone out with a rancher from the next county who had an unfortunate fondness for chewing tobacco, then a slightly older widower who hadn't gotten over his deceased wife. A cowboy she'd met at a rodeo in Billings had lasted a few weeks. But they hadn't clicked well enough to make a long-distance relationship work. Her mother hinted that Melanie was too picky. That was partly true. She'd never settle for the sake of a gold band on her finger. But it was also laughable since she doubted her parents would approve of half the men she found appealing.

She wondered what they'd think of someone like Lucas. He obviously had a generous heart. She assumed he was a volunteer for Prison Reform Now. But even if he held a paid position, a man doing that job wasn't looking to get rich.

Hefting a bag of feed off the flatbed, he flashed her a smile.

A soft gasp escaped her. Without realizing, she'd actually stopped and was staring again. Nearly tripping over herself, she hurried to the office. Once inside, she planted her butt in the chair behind the desk and waited for her heart rate to slow down.

Seconds later she got up and slanted the blinds, but the window was in the wrong position. She couldn't see much of him. Probably just as well. She had a lot of work to tackle, and though Lucas was nice eye candy, he'd be gone in an hour or so. And Blackfoot Falls would be the same boring town that she'd woken up to this morning.

LUCAS WOULD'VE PREFERRED to shower before meeting with the pretty schoolteacher. Though she, of all people, understood why he might be a little ripe. Damn, he was glad he'd helped Levi. The guy had a weak back and bad arthritis. No way should he be doing that kind of manual work. But as Levi had confided, if not him, Kathy and Melanie would have done the unloading, which happened often enough. And they were both small women.

He paused at the office door and knocked, even though Levi had told him to just walk in. Melanie called that it was open, just as she'd done earlier, and why that made him smile he had no idea. Maybe it was the trace of impatience in her voice. She seemed the type who'd be appalled that she'd let it show.

Melanie got up as he entered, and she moved a box that was sitting on the spare chair. Then she went to the small fridge. Oddly, he felt his body tighten. Just because he knew she had to bend over? That was pretty damn sad.

"Water or cola?" she asked.

"Water." He ordered himself not to look and did anyway. Different jeans than before. These were a bit snugger. A-plus for the teacher. "Thanks."

She'd brought out a bottle for herself, too, and hid behind the old desk again. "You're the one who deserves my thanks. Levi is terrific, never complains. He does most of the heavy lifting, even when he shouldn't."

"Yeah, he told me about the arthritis."

"Did he?" She seemed surprised. "Normally, he doesn't like to talk about it."

"How many volunteers do you have?"

"Seven who come rain or shine, including Shea and myself, Kathy and Levi. Another four we can usually count on to show up twice a week or if we're in a tight spot. A few more pitch in but not with any regularity."

"Mostly women, I take it?"

Melanie nodded. "Now, if we have an emergency or the weather is bad, the McAllister brothers are here in a heartbeat. They own a big ranch to the south of town and have their hands full but they've never let us down. Shea moved here because of Jesse, the middle brother, who's also a pilot. He's flown air rescue for so many animals that wouldn't have made it if not for him."

"Safe Haven owns a plane?"

"No," she said, drawing out the word with a laugh. "Until this spring the coffers were so empty it's a miracle this place held together. We went nonprofit and were lucky enough to get some serious funding." A small impish smile lifted her lips. "It doesn't hurt that the former director just married a man with a sizable charitable foundation."

"Ah." Lucas had no trouble smiling back. She was different from the women he usually dealt with inside the organization.

Like Melanie, they were volunteers. They were also members of Denver's elite. They had money, influence, time on their hands and, most of them, a legitimate interest in prison reform. No question the wheels would move a lot slower without their support. But their generosity had clear limitations. They gladly opened their checkbooks, made phone calls to people who mattered, talked up the cause at their fancy cocktail parties, but their hands always managed to stay clean.

Melanie swept the hair away from her face and blinked at him. "I guess we should get to the reason you're here."

"I assume you know the basics. I emailed some material about our group and what we're trying to accomplish."

"Yes," she said, nodding thoughtfully. "If I understand correctly, the program is a collaborative effort between the state and the prison system. A portion of the wild horses gathered by the government each year are sent to the prison farms, and the inmates train the animals, which are then auctioned off, with the money that's raised going back to the prison."

"In a nutshell, yes."

"The program is self-supporting and appears to be very successful." She paused. "I did glance at the material you sent, but I'm not as prepared as I should be and for that I apologize. But why would a private group like PRN be involved?"

"Various state laws and budgets dictate who gets what. We'd like to see the program spread around." Lucas liked that she was interested and didn't hesitate to ask questions. Hell, he liked *her.* "Tell you what…apology accepted." He held back a smile at her raised brows. "But only if you have dinner with me."

3

"DINNER?" SHE JUST LAUGHED. "You do realize that most people in your position—i.e., you wanting something from us—would say, 'No apology necessary. I appreciate your time.'"

"Okay." A smile tugged at his mouth. "Should I try again? I can do that. Trouble is, I'm starving. Haven't eaten since I left Wyoming this morning. I don't think well on an empty stomach."

"I see." A nervous tingling sensation started low in her belly. It was his eyes. The way he was looking at her... Was he flirting? She couldn't think with him watching her like that. "Well, you did help Levi, so I guess I should feed you."

His expression shifted, as if he'd mentally taken a giant step back. "Unless you have plans, I figured we can talk and eat at the same time." He shrugged. "Or not. I can wait."

She felt her composure falter. Had she just scared him with a wrong signal? He was merely being practical, and she was being an idiot. Dinner made sense. It didn't mean he wanted her company. "There's a diner in town."

"Is the food good?"

"Fortunately, yes, since that's the only option. Well, the Food Mart has a deli counter, some ready-made items. They even have a few tables and chairs if you want to eat there." Oh, that was a stupid suggestion. It would be crowded with people she knew—most of them nosy.

"I like the deli idea."

"Be warned, it's not a real deli. Not like you'd find in Denver."

Lucas smiled. "I grew up in a town similar to Blackfoot Falls."

"How big?"

"Maybe three thousand people in the entire county."

"Same here. A few people live in town, but mostly ranching families and hired hands make up the population. They're spread out for miles."

"Yep. I understand."

"So you know what that means…."

He gave the matter a moment's thought and then sighed. "Everyone who walks into the Food Mart will want to know who I am and what we're talking about."

"Some might even pull up a chair."

"Yeah." He rubbed his jaw. "We're not gonna do that."

"No. Bad idea."

"What about picking up food and eating outside? I bet you know a few good picnic spots."

"Um, a picnic?" That didn't sound at all businesslike. She grabbed her water and took a hearty sip.

"Okay. I see that was a miss. Guess it's the diner."

"No, no, it's not a…" She sighed. "You know what…. A picnic sounds great, no interruptions," she said, trying to recall what food she still had stashed in the old cabin. "We might not have to pick up anything from town." She stood. "Take a walk with me."

He quickly got to his feet and opened the door for her. "Where are we going?"

"Just over there," she said, stepping outside and gesturing to the tiny hovel of a cabin. "The former director used to live there."

Lucas frowned. "I'd be claustrophobic."

"It has a loft that was used for a bedroom. But you're right—I couldn't have done it. Plus, it doubled as an office. That would've been okay, but not living there, too." She nodded at the large cabin to the right of the gravel path. "The new place has three bedrooms and two baths. The electrician still has to come out, but it's very nice. Now we just need a director."

"Any bites?"

"Kathy and Levi were the front-runners. But their children moved south with their families. Kathy misses them. She and Levi will be making a move themselves eventually. And frankly, with Levi's recent health problems, this place would be too much."

"What about you?"

The question surprised her. She turned to look at him. He was awfully close. Close enough for her to see his pupils dilate. She took a quick breath. "Believe it or not, teaching keeps me quite busy."

"It's kind of a shame.... You seem like a good fit. But then, you're also the kind of teacher these kids need."

Melanie stopped outside the door of the old cabin and gave him a quizzical look. He didn't know her....

"Your students explained how you got them involved here. Told me about the alternative agricultural methods you guys are exploring. Growing your own alfalfa to make Safe Haven more self-sustaining? Really impressive. So is getting them school credit to volunteer."

Surprised, she blinked. "I see they were quite chatty. Anything else?"

He smiled. "Only that you couldn't decide between being a teacher or a vet."

"Gee, did they tell you what color underwear I prefer?"

"Uh, no," he said, the skin at the corners of his eyes crinkling with amusement. "We didn't get to that."

She shook her head, laughing and groaning at the same time, and tried the doorknob. It had always stuck, but with the lack of frequent use, it was more stubborn than usual.

"Let me try." Lucas took over, but he hadn't left room for her to get out of the way.

He put his shoulder into the effort, and she stared at the rippling motion of his muscles flexing and releasing. His elbow grazed her right breast, and she tensed. He didn't seem to notice or else purposely ignored the contact. Her nipples tightened, and she realized that in her hurry to squeeze in a shower, she'd forgotten to wear a T-shirt bra.

The door opened, startling her into taking a step backward on the uneven ground. Lucas steadied her with his large hand briefly on her arm. The frantic pace of her pulse really annoyed her. She wasn't going down that road again. This was business and she really wasn't *that* starved for a man's attention. No, that was a lie. She'd been suffering a drought for a while now. Usually she was just better at ignoring it.

"Yep, it's a tight space."

She followed his gaze to the battered old recliner pushed against the wall and the small scarred table Annie had used as a desk and for everything else. The kitchen was nothing more than a sink and a counter with a microwave, a toaster oven and a coffeepot. Underneath was a mini fridge on its last legs.

"I don't know how Annie managed," Melanie said and moved inside. "The loft has a bed, a small dresser and that's it. But the worst thing is the tiny shower. It's almost criminal."

Lucas ducked his head, spotted the door to the bathroom tucked under the stairs. "How long did she live here?"

"Two years."

He let out a low whistle. "That's dedication."

"There isn't a word for how hard Annie worked. Without her the sanctuary would've folded by now."

He joined her at the counter, where she was looking through a plastic bin of dry goods. "Won't be easy for anyone to follow in her footsteps."

The cabin felt even smaller with him standing so close. "I wouldn't even try. I'm not that selfless," she said, grabbing a box of crackers. "Still, Shea and I are willing to go to any lengths not to let Annie down."

"Understood," he said, his faint smile indicating he'd taken her words as a warning.

She averted her gaze and returned to inventorying their picnic options.

"Peanut butter." He picked up the jar she'd set beside the crackers, studying it as if he'd struck gold. "Man, I haven't had this in years."

"I wouldn't last two weeks without peanut butter."

"I ate it every day when I first bought the ranch. The old place needed so much work I was too exhausted to shop or cook." He started to twist the cap. "You mind?"

"Go for it." She smiled when he got the top off and took a big whiff. "Where's your ranch?"

"Wyoming."

That surprised her. She'd assumed he lived somewhere near Denver, where Prison Reform Now was headquartered. She brought out deli turkey and cheese and mayonnaise from the fridge. Two apples were left over from the other day, so she grabbed them, too. She straightened and saw him searching the counter. Assuming he wanted a knife, she handed him one.

He dipped it into the jar, scooped out a mound of peanut butter and offered it to her. She shook her head, and he used his finger to sweep the whole glob into his mouth.

Melanie grinned. "Okay, I might be going out on a limb here…but I'm thinking we can skip the trip to town."

Looking like a kid trying not to talk with his mouth full, Lucas nodded enthusiastically. He pointed to the food and gave her a thumbs-up.

Okay, she didn't need him looking that adorable. What she did need, however, was a dose of common sense. She'd bag the food and take it to the office. No reason they couldn't eat there. "How about a horseback ride?" she asked instead, evidently channeling Chelsea, which was a terrifying thought. "I know just the spot."

He agreed, so she gathered their dinner, while he found napkins and washed the knife. It would have been downright cozy if she hadn't been caught stealing looks at him. Of course, she'd caught him looking back.

When Kathy saw them saddling the horses, she gave her a blanket and a wink. Melanie volleyed with a glare normally reserved for boys who loitered outside the girls' locker room. Thank goodness Lucas had missed the exchange. But that hadn't stopped her from blushing like a lunatic.

The silent ten-minute ride went quickly and comfortably, considering the storm brewing in Melanie's head. The sun was sinking, the air wasn't too warm, and in fact, the crisp breeze hitting her cheeks felt refreshing. It would've been perfect if only her mind hadn't kept circling back to the same question. What on earth was she doing? They couldn't have that much to discuss. It would've made more sense to have eaten in the office while they talked and then gone their separate ways. She still had a lot of work to do. He probably had a long drive to wherever he was going next.

And yet she wasn't sorry. She didn't feel bad for not doing the sensible thing. She was enjoying Lucas. That wasn't a crime or a sin. Though to ignore the broad stretch of his T-shirt across his shoulders might be.

"Is that it?" He pointed to the grassy knoll protected by a thicket of aspens.

"How did you know?"

"That's where I'd go." He twisted around in his saddle and looked back toward Blackfoot Falls and the distant Rockies. "Great view."

"You can even see part of Safe Haven."

He swung off Sergei, the gelding he'd chosen, and tethered the black to a sapling.

Before she could dismount, Lucas caught her by the waist and helped her down. She shoved the hair out of her eyes, about to tell him he didn't need to do that, but he had strong hands and all she could manage was "Thanks."

He smiled and turned his attention to the mare. "Is she your favorite?" he asked and stroked the horse's neck.

"Candy Cane is everyone's favorite. Someone abandoned her two years ago. Can you imagine? She's so sweet and gentle I never worry when the kids want to ride her."

"I'm surprised you haven't found her a home."

Melanie grinned at the mare, who nudged Lucas with her muzzle when he stopped stroking her to gather the reins. "You shameless hussy," Melanie said, taking over pampering duty as they walked to the sapling. "Safe Haven is her home now. We've never tried to place her."

His thoughtful frown warned her that he'd switched to business mode. "Last year I heard you had to move close to a hundred horses because you were overcrowded."

Nodding, she watched him tether Candy next to Sergei. "Annie was still here then. It was bad. No funds, very little feed to get through winter. Luckily, two other sanctuaries took them in."

"Some were mustangs that eventually ended up in the prison system." He collected the blanket, and she grabbed their dinner. "That's how we learned about Safe Haven. Your operation is small and out of the way, so you hadn't been on our radar."

"Small? Are you kidding? Sometimes it feels as though we're drowning." She stopped in the shade, though the sun was low and weak. "I'm not complaining—"

"I know. You don't have someone here full-time, and you and Shea have other jobs. Volunteers mean well but you can't count on them. This is a remote area, so new volunteers aren't coming out of the woodwork. And with this economy, donations are down. I get it." He shook out the blanket. "Yet look at what you two are accomplishing in spite of everything."

"No, not me. I have limited involvement. It's people like Kathy and Levi—" She watched him crouch to smooth out the wool blanket, smiling. "What?"

"You're being modest."

"I am not."

He took the bag of food from her and set it down. "I like the way you think outside the box. What you're doing with your students is commendable." He studied her for a moment. "Did you grow up here?"

"Yes."

"On a ranch?"

"No, not really. We always had a few animals. Mostly chickens, two mares, a milking cow…"

"You're teaching those kids valuable life skills. And they're learning to have a healthy respect for animals. You'd think that wouldn't need to be taught. That any decent human being would understand their responsibility to—" He stopped, cleared his throat and looked away.

His voice had sounded strained; his jaw was still clenched. The blue eyes she'd found so appealing had turned cold, sending a shiver straight down her spine. He kept his gaze averted and stared at the Rockies—to hide the sudden darkness that had come over him, she suspected. She was guessing he'd had a bad experience with someone mistreating an animal. That was enough to push her buttons.

She moved closer. He was a stranger, a man she'd met only a few hours ago. What was wrong with her that she didn't feel some modicum of fear? Did she have no survival instincts at all? His tension all but blasted her like heat from a furnace. His mouth was tight-lipped and grim, cautioning her to give him space. And yet the warning had an opposite effect.

The curse she'd hidden since hitting puberty was to blame. That was the only explanation. Why else would quiet Melanie, Pastor Ray's obedient daughter, feel this stirring inside her, feel a deep longing to touch Lucas? Good girls stayed away from bad boys. They didn't go looking for trouble.

She hesitated, giving herself a final chance to sync with reason, but it was no use. She touched his arm.

He slowly turned and glanced at her hand. "Sorry, did you say something?"

For the life of her, she couldn't come up with an excuse for touching him. Or for standing this close. She moved her hand to her side and focused on the Big Belt Mountains. "Would you like me to point out landmarks? There's Mount Edith over there. And on the right—"

Lightly brushing the back of her hand, he said, "How about we eat?"

She curled her fingers into her cold palm. And then realized he hadn't initiated contact at all. Her trembling hand had grazed his. Keeping her gaze averted, she inched away. "Sure, let's— I'll set out the food."

He caught her wrist, just to get her attention, then released her. "I got carried away there," he said. "I'm sorry I frightened you."

"You didn't." She shook her head. "I was concerned."

She rubbed her arms and saw the skepticism in his faint smile. "Okay, and maybe a teensy bit nervous."

His mouth lifted in earnest, and just like that, there was the man who'd changed the bus tire. "Are you always this forthright?"

"I try to be."

"No matter what the consequences?"

"I'd like to think so," she said, mesmerized by his bold stare. The demons were gone, if that was what had drawn him briefly into darkness. Now he just looked curious. "You sound so serious. Please tell me you aren't setting me up to play Truth or Dare."

He laughed at that. "I've never played and don't want to know how."

She relaxed and smiled, surprised that for a second she'd been afraid he'd admit something she didn't want to know. Something that might change her opinion of him. Which was crazy. She barely knew him. "It's just a dumb college pastime also known as study avoidance."

She needed to move, not just stand there staring at him. To stay put would invite him to…

His gaze dropped to her mouth, and her pulse leaped.

SHE STOOD THERE, watching him with a mix of want and fear. This was…unexpected. Different from the way the Chelseas of the world eyed him like a stud up for auction.

Lucas had first started seeing that look as a teenager and had been quick to take advantage of it. But he wasn't that reckless, carefree kid anymore, and a woman like Melanie? He stayed clear of women like her.

He could tell she was a nice small-town girl. Curious about him but uncertain what she wanted. He might've been out of circulation for a while and still a little rusty, but some things a man didn't forget. Like the look of a woman who wanted to be kissed or silky skin and a soft mouth. He'd bet Melanie tasted real sweet. She'd likely be a little timid at first, but not for long.

Those thoughts had to stop. If he had a shred of decency left in him, he'd leave her alone. Leave her exactly how he'd found her when he eventually drove away from Blackfoot Falls. She wasn't anything like the women he'd slept with in Denver, the rich ones affiliated with the reform program. Hell, he'd been nothing more than a novelty to them. It hadn't taken long to figure that out. Not that that was a deal breaker. Uncomplicated sex was all he wanted or expected from a woman. He couldn't say why, but he had a feeling that sex with Melanie would be anything but simple.

She finally turned away, knelt on the blanket and started setting out their picnic. He didn't miss the slump of her shoulders or the blush staining her cheeks.

He crouched beside her. "Need help?"

"I think I can handle this. Here." She offered him water.

A beer would've been more to his liking but he took the bottle. "Is there a bar in town?"

"I doubt there's a ranching community in this country that doesn't have at least one."

"I don't know.... There might be a few dry counties left."

"Huh. The Watering Hole is the go-to place for the local ranch hands. Some prefer to head over to Kalispell, but I can't imagine them not having someplace close to blow off steam."

"Is the Watering Hole where you go?"

"Me?" She laughed. "No."

"You telling me teachers don't need to unwind or vent?"

"Oh, we have student voodoo dolls for that."

Lucas smiled. "What else?" He watched her try to shake free a stray curl that clung to her cheek. Since her hands were full, he tucked the lock behind her ear. "What do you do, Melanie?" he asked, reluctant to lower his hand. Her skin and hair were as soft as he'd imagined. "To relieve the pressure?"

"I guess I'm lucky," she said, a trace of huskiness in her voice. "I'm always too exhausted to think about it."

He took the mayonnaise from her. "Not good. Stress seems to have a habit of turning the tables one way or another." He opened the jar and set it aside.

"What do *you* do?" She busied herself with pulling napkins and silverware out of the bag. "You have to travel and meet new people, lobby for their help. It might be rewarding but I can't imagine it's fun."

"No, most times it isn't. As a rule people don't care about prisoners. They figure inmates are getting what they deserve."

"I can understand the bias. Do folks ever worry about the safety of the horses?"

"I've been asked that more than a few times." He noticed the small frown forming between her brows. "Is that your concern?"

"No, not at all. I mean, of course I know everyone in prison *claims* they're innocent," she said with a small dismissive shrug. "But no, I'm not worried."

He smiled despite the twist in his gut. "Some prisoners actually *are* innocent."

Too bad he hadn't been one of them.

4

AFTER THEY'D EATEN and the leftovers had been stowed, Melanie glanced at her watch. Lucas had explained more about the Wild Horse Training Program, and so far she saw no reason why Safe Haven couldn't participate. All PRN wanted to do was use the sanctuary as a stopgap between the gathers and moving the horses to the various prisons. It wouldn't cost Safe Haven anything. Food, transportation, even manpower would be completely covered. Not only that, but PRN might be interested in taking some of the strays Melanie had been unable to adopt out. Naturally, she had to lay out everything for Shea so they could make the decision together, but Prison Reform Now seemed to be very well funded.

What did concern her was the time. Another hour and it would start getting dark, though Lucas didn't seem to be worried.

She watched him straighten the wool blanket, then sit down again so that he faced the orange glow of the sun sinking behind the Rockies. What she'd expected him to do was roll up the blanket and stuff it into the saddlebag along with their sack of trash.

Her gaze fell on his rounded biceps, then followed the

cords of muscle to his wrist. He didn't wear a watch. And though she knew he carried a cell phone, he hadn't brought it out once. If he wasn't anxious to get on the road, then why should she care?

No denying she was enjoying herself. The fresh air was nice and the quiet soothing. Working at Safe Haven was rewarding but seldom relaxing. Between grading papers and doing the shopping and cooking for two elderly church members, Melanie rarely had a moment for herself.

Of course, rounding out her enjoyment was Lucas, and that distant enigmatic expression of his. She'd seen it twice now, and goodness, it wasn't easy keeping the naughty fantasies at bay. She refused to guess at his dark thoughts or imagine him as a teenager. He would've been one of those brooding guys the girls whispered about to their friends and dreamed about at night. The type of guy who'd always been and would always be out of reach for a quiet, sensible woman like her.

She realized she'd sighed out loud when he looked up and caught her staring at him. Quickly she cleared her throat. "We should go. We don't have much daylight left," she said, feeling even more awkward standing next to Candy Cane and peering down at him as if he were one of her pupils.

A lazy smile curved his mouth. He arched back, stretching out his arms, then pushed to his feet with the agility of a teenager. "You're right. I've monopolized enough of your time."

"No, it's not that—I assumed you'd want to get on the road before nightfall."

"I'm not leaving yet," he said and scooped up the blanket. "I figured I'd spend a few days here."

"Oh."

"Is that a problem?"

"No." She nodded. "Maybe."

"Which is it?" The corners of his mouth twitched, which she saw quite clearly since he'd sidled up next to her. "Give me a hint."

"Okay, smarty." Inwardly cringing at using the silly word, she resisted the urge to move over. "Did you drive through town?"

"Yes," he said, "and judging by your smug expression, I assume I missed something."

It wasn't easy being this close and feeling the heat from his body. Part of her wanted to lean into him; the other part was already yanking her shirt backward. "Did you see any motels?"

He kept looking at her, his right brow lifting. "A place called the Boarding House."

"It's not a motel. It really was a boardinghouse about ninety years ago."

Lucas frowned. "There were cars parked out front."

"Someone just bought the place and is making it an inn." She tried to look innocent. "I doubt it'll be finished by tonight."

He let out a laugh. "I underestimated you."

"I'm sorry—I shouldn't be teasing."

"So there's really no lodging in Blackfoot Falls?"

"None."

"The closest place to get a room would be—where? Kalispell?"

"That's right," she said, not feeling the least triumphant. She wanted him to stay longer. "There is one other possibility," she said slowly, trying to think it through.

She could call Rachel at the Sundance. The dude ranch was usually booked months in advance but there was a chance they could somehow make room for Lucas. She'd ask as a personal favor if she had to. Or was she being foolish?

"Melanie?"

She met his expectant gaze.

He waited and after a few moments said, "If you're offering me your guest room—"

Her gasp interrupted him. "Me? No, I don't have— I mean, I do have a spare room, but I live in town. I have neighbors." She felt the heat sting her cheeks and there was nothing she could do about it. "Very nosy neighbors, and it's not that I care about what they say. It's just— Well, no, I do care but—"

"Melanie." He touched her arm to stop her rambling.

After taking a deep breath, she managed a smile. It felt brittle and fake. "Sorry, that came out wrong."

His hand moved to her face. Her burning-hot face. Just in case he needed proof of her embarrassment.

Oh, Lord.

"Don't be sorry," he murmured. "I was teasing you, and it was inappropriate. And even if you offered, I wouldn't take you up on it."

Her humiliation sank to another low. "No, of course not. We just met. Why would you?"

Lucas looked as if he was trying to control a smile. "Having just met you doesn't bother me. Small town, you being a teacher. No matter how innocent the situation, I know it would be bad for you. I wouldn't want that."

She searched his eyes, unsure what she was looking for, and he eventually lowered his hand. It wasn't relief she felt but disappointment. Dammit, she wanted him to kiss her. She wanted to kiss him. She knew it would mean nothing to him, if he even responded, and she didn't care.

He turned away to deal with the blanket, struggling to roll up the bulky wool, and she started to lose her nerve. And then it occurred to her that she'd never initiated a kiss. Not once. Ever. She'd been willing plenty of times when a date had taken the lead. But here she was, twenty-seven, two semi-long-term college relationships behind her, and she'd never kissed a boy first. Wow, that was kind of sad.

"Lucas?"

He looked over and automatically smiled.

Swallowing back a lump of nerves, she moved closer. "Need help?"

"Sure." He'd brought two corners together. "Take this end."

Melanie obliged, gripping the blanket, spreading her arms wide and moving backward while he scooped up the lower corners. If he'd guessed at her cowardly gear switching, he didn't let on. She hadn't given up on the kiss yet. Just looking for a more organic way to swoop in.

Oh, who was she kidding? It would be awkward for her no matter what. She was still willing to try, though. Nervous as she was, it was clear this was one of those times she'd regret being harmless as a pet rabbit, as her grandfather used to say.

"You have to stop."

She blinked. "Stop what?"

"Moving."

"Right." She laughed when she realized that he'd had to move along with her or lose his grip. "I was daydreaming. Sorry."

The light seemed to be slipping quickly all of a sudden. Before long the twilight shadows would start playing tricks. Already Lucas's seductive eyes had turned a deeper shade of blue as he walked the few feet to join her.

"You can let go," he said, taking her corners.

About to protest they could do better as a team, she closed her mouth and watched him fold the more manageable half into thirds, then smaller. He finished the task with startling precision. Very neatly he slid the compacted blanket into the saddlebag.

"Were you in the military?"

Shaking his head, he finished securing the saddlebag, then turned to her. "Why do you ask?"

"You're so neat."

"My mom could've been a drill sergeant. Does that count?"

"So could mine, though not as successfully as yours," she said drily and glanced up at the sky. It was clear overhead. Toward the Belt Mountains and Rockies, salmony-pink clouds shrouded the peaks. She loved sunsets and really needed to take more time to enjoy them. "The Sundance ranch takes in guests," she said, noting that Lucas had been watching her. No reason to get nervous, she told herself and walked over to untie their horses. "I can call to see if they have room for you. Jesse McAllister, the man I mentioned earlier… His family owns the ranch."

"A dude ranch?"

"Yes and no. They're cattlemen. The family have raised cattle on that land for generations, but times are tough. They have a lot of hired hands to keep working, so they expanded, did what they had to do."

"Good for them."

"If there's any chance they can put you up, they will. I know them. Really terrific people."

"If it's no trouble, yeah, I'd appreciate you making the call." He paused. "Hey, what about the old cabin? In exchange I'll make a donation to Safe Haven."

"Annie's cabin? The one that made you claustrophobic?"

He shrugged. "It beats driving all the way to Kalispell tonight."

Discovering that he didn't intend to leave town over inconvenient accommodations pleased her more than was warranted. "Unfortunately, a couple of volunteers are using it tonight. But it should be free tomorrow," she said, holding out the gelding's reins.

Lucas made a move to take them, only he didn't. He

closed his hand over hers. "Tell me if I'm wrong, but it seems you've been dying to say something." His voice was so low and compelling she almost didn't notice that he was drawing her closer. "Do you have something to tell me, Melanie?"

She felt his warm breath on her chin, and her mind went blank. Blood raced through her veins and roared in her ears. "Thank you for fixing the tire."

He didn't laugh or mock her for being a coward. But he knew. "Is that all?"

To her surprise, she glimpsed a shadow of uncertainty in his eyes. Not trusting her voice, she slowly shook her head.

"I'm not going anywhere." He'd released her hand but their arms still touched. "I've got all night."

Go on, you chicken, make the move. He's waiting.

"I think I should call the Sundance as soon as possible," she said, completely disgusted with herself.

Briefly searching her face, he gave her a faint smile and started to turn.

"Wait." She pushed herself at him, pressing her palm against his chest, putting her other hand on his shoulder. Stretching up on her toes, she brushed her lips across his mouth.

His lack of response sent panic and embarrassment spiraling through her. How could she have read him so wrong? Before she could flee, he pulled her into his arms. His mouth came down on hers, and she froze in surprise.

His fingers cupped the back of her neck while his warm lips moved across her mouth. He tightened his arm around her lower back, and she felt herself begin to yield to the soft gentle tugs at her lips. Just as she was about to open for him, he drew back and looked at her.

"You want me to stop?" he asked, studying her closely.

"No." She understood the problem. Her initial shock had come across as resistance. "No, I don't."

He started kneading the tense muscles at the back of her neck, his light erotic touch relaxing her. She felt her chin dropping to her chest and couldn't seem to stop it. He nudged it back up, then cupped her head with both hands and slipped his tongue between her parted lips.

Everything inside her melted. His mouth was warm, damp and skillful, and he took his time, erasing any doubt. He ran his hands down her back, pulling her against his body, and she started to tremble. She'd always liked kissing well enough, but when Lucas touched his tongue to hers, then lazily swept her mouth, a slow aching burn in the pit of her stomach started, an ache she'd never felt before.

She could feel him hardening against her belly, could feel her heart race, could feel her nipples tighten. His mouth wasn't so gentle anymore. She understood his growing hunger. She clutched his shoulders, wanting more, wanting him to quench that burn of longing that flared hotter but not sure how to ask for it. Or even if she should. A kiss was one thing....

She swayed a little, and he pulled back to look at her. She blinked, trying to focus. He brushed another kiss across her lips and released her.

"That wasn't planned," he murmured, "but I won't apologize."

"I'd be annoyed if you did."

Lucas smiled. "If I'd had a teacher like you, high school might not have been so painful."

Melanie stiffened, then turned to hide her reaction. She was a teacher and to some degree a role model. But she had a right to a private life. It wasn't as if she made a habit of kissing good-looking strangers, and certainly not in front of her students. No, it was the "stranger" part that had her shaken. And on her home turf. Clearly she was overworked.

"So you didn't like school, huh?" she said, unnecessarily cinching Candy's saddle strap. He'd tasted faintly of peanut butter, and the lingering flavor on her own lips calmed her, fooled her into thinking he was more familiar.

"I hated sitting indoors all day. What you're doing for these kids by bringing them out here shouldn't be underestimated. I bet they learn more by being involved with the sanctuary."

Delighted by his observation, she turned back to him. "A few parents objected at first. I think they equated coming out here to field trips instead of an actual learning experience. But now, as long as this doesn't interfere with football practice, everyone's okay with it." The corners of his mouth quirked up. "What?"

"Don't like football, huh?"

She shrugged. "It's okay, I guess. I don't really have an opinion about it."

"You rolled your eyes."

"Did I? Just now?"

Watching her, Lucas nodded. "I bet you fought like a tiger for the program."

How could she not be aware of rolling her eyes? She didn't like that, not one bit. She prided herself on remaining centered, keeping her expressions impassive, especially when dealing with the students and their parents. And especially with her father's congregation. Even when she disagreed with his dogma.

"Melanie?"

She blinked at him. "I doubt I was that fierce. But yes, I felt strongly about bringing the classroom outside. Some of the kids will be moving to cities, but a lot of them will end up taking over the family ranch. They need to know they have other options and not just do what their parents and grandparents have done."

A slight frown drew his brows together, as if she confused him. Though she couldn't imagine why. She was straightforward and predictable, much more likely to inspire a yawn than confusion.

"A tiger?" she said and turned to Candy when the mare moved restlessly. "That was a strange analogy."

"Why?" He watched her mount, then swung into his own saddle. "You strike me as someone who would go all out for something they believed in."

"Really?"

"Why are you surprised?"

She led him past the thicket of aspens, wondering how on earth he'd gotten that impression. Obviously he was seeing something that just wasn't there. She rarely made waves, whether at school or at church. Occasionally she might tweak the status quo, but no one would accuse her of hoisting the rebel flag.

Heck, she hated that her neighbor hung wet rugs on the shared picket fence that was now beginning to sag from the weight. But Melanie hadn't said a word to Mrs. Sutter.

Anxious to let the subject drop, she dug her phone out of her pocket, then glanced back at him. "I'll call the Sundance if you're still interested in staying overnight."

"If it's not a problem."

"Calling the Sundance?"

"Me staying." Lucas tried to hold her gaze as he rode up alongside her, but she looked away.

"No, of course not. Why would it be—?" She knew better than to ask a question that could produce an answer she might not like. She hit speed dial and prayed for the call to go through. Up here the reception could be dicey.

The connection dropped after the third ring. She kept the phone to her ear while she gathered her composure.

The weird thing about him having misread her was that Lucas was observant. The kind of quiet, intense observant that made her nervous. Made her feel self-conscious, as if she needed to explain herself.

She knew he didn't mean to upset her. After living under a magnifying glass half her life, she could tell the difference. And she also knew he was watching her right now.

"Oops." She lowered the cell phone. "Lost the call. I'll have to try again in a few minutes."

He gazed up at the sky. "If they don't have room, I keep a sleeping bag in my truck. Looks like a nice night to sleep under the stars."

"You'd do that?"

"Sure." He glanced at her. "I love sleeping outdoors. Only problem is I gotta have my morning shower."

A stunningly vivid picture of him wet and naked flashed in her mind. She let out a gasp that startled them both. What was wrong with her?

"Not a fan of outdoor living, I take it," he said, amusement lacing his tone.

"Um, no, I've enjoyed camping, but yeah, the, um, shower thing..." She cleared her throat and hit speed dial again. "That's a deal breaker for me."

She'd never been so glad to hear Rachel's voice. "Hey, it's Melanie. I know it's last-minute, but have you got an extra room?"

"Actually, we do," Rachel said. "But only for one night. We have a ton of arrivals tomorrow. Who's it for?"

Melanie gave Lucas an affirming nod, and then it dawned on her. "Oh, wait, do you accept male guests?"

He was looking at her, his eyes narrowed and curious.

Rachel laughed. "Yeah, sure, but you'll have to warn him. You know how some of these women are." She lowered her voice. "Subtle as a mare in heat."

Letting out a chuckle, Melanie briefly met his eyes. "He looks pretty tough. I think he can handle them."

"Hey, you giggled. Who is this guy?"

Melanie groaned. "Goodbye, Rachel, and thank you."

"Wait—"

Melanie disconnected the call but didn't bother pocketing the phone. Rachel was probably already texting her little heart out. "There's room for you at the Sundance but only for one night," she told Lucas without looking at him, because her pink cheeks would only invite more curiosity. "If you're still interested in sticking around, we can see if the cabin's available tomorrow."

"I'm interested." He nudged Sergei to keep up with her and Candy Cane. "I think."

"You can decide tomorrow," Melanie said, pleased at her cool even tone. Despite the dreaded thought he could change his mind and leave first thing in the morning.

"Is there something you should tell me?"

She turned to him. "Like what?"

A small cautious smile curved his mouth. "You asked if your friend takes male guests."

"Oh." Her phone buzzed. No surprise, it was a text from Rachel. "Excuse me—I think this is about your reservation," she murmured, assuring herself she hadn't lied.

WTF? CALL ME THE SEC HE LEAVES.

Melanie hurriedly stuffed the phone in her pocket. "You're all set."

"Are you purposely trying to make me nervous?"

"No, of course not…." She saw he was kidding. Duh. It probably took an earthquake to rattle him. "The Sundance sort of caters to young single women."

"Sort of?"

"They'll be crawling all over the place."

"Great." He sighed, clearly not pleased.

And that suited Melanie just fine.

5

LUCAS STEPPED ONTO the porch of the McAllisters' large three-story log house carrying his bag, the brim of his Stetson tugged down low. Normally, he wouldn't have bothered wearing his hat from his truck to the front door. But it helped eliminate unnecessary eye contact.

He'd assumed Melanie had exaggerated about the ranch being overrun by female guests. Hell, he must've seen two dozen of them already, and he'd only just arrived. Fortunately, it seemed most of the ladies were headed to the row of rental cars parked near the stable. Though that hadn't stopped a few from trying to engage him in conversation.

The door opened before he could knock.

"Hi, you must be Lucas." The woman had long auburn curls, bright green eyes and a friendly smile. "I'm Rachel McAllister. Come in."

He saw a trio of women approaching from behind her, and he automatically stepped to the side.

Rachel glanced over her shoulder. "I think this is the last wave," she whispered, then moved to let the women pass.

The curvy brunette and her smaller friend flashed him smiles as they walked past him and hurried down the porch steps. A tall blonde wearing red heels and a short denim skirt lagged behind them, pausing to say something to Rachel that made her laugh.

"My brothers are spoken for," Rachel said. "You see them in town, you leave them alone. Same goes for Matt."

"You know I'm harmless." The blonde gave her a mischievous grin, then continued onto the porch. She stopped again when she spotted Lucas. Eyeing him up and down, she drawled, "I haven't seen you before."

"Nope, just got here." He had a good look at her ample breasts. Couldn't miss them, molded by the clingy shirt.

She let her gaze drift down to his bag, then made the trip back up his jeans to his face, her blue eyes frank and challenging. "Are you checking in?"

"I am." He touched the brim of his hat. "You have a nice evening."

Her brows lifted, partly in surprise but mostly in irritation. A woman like her rarely got turned down. Any other night, he might've been interested. Not now. He was tired and anxious to hear more about Safe Haven from the McAllisters. Maybe even learn something about Melanie.

"See you in the morning, Angela." Rachel motioned for him to enter.

Angela clearly wasn't happy about being dismissed but she gave him a slight shrug, then continued down the steps to join her friends.

"I hope Mel warned you that we cater to women," Rachel said, closing the door as soon as he crossed into the foyer. "Maybe you don't mind the attention, which is fine, too." She gave him a subtle once-over herself, but only out of curiosity. "Everyone else is at the Watering Hole in town or in Kalispell."

Lucas smiled and removed his hat. "I'd prefer the peace and quiet."

"Good." She smiled back. "I'll take you to your room. You can leave your bag, wash up, whatever, then I'll show you the kitchen. We have leftover short ribs, chicken and potatoes, maybe some peach cobbler. There's a pool table in the den, if you're interested. Also a fridge stocked with beer and soft drinks."

"Shouldn't we settle up first?" he said when she headed for the stairs. "I'm not sure how early I'll be checking out."

She stopped on the first step. "Oh, please. I'm not taking your money. You're a friend of Safe Haven. We're happy to put you up."

"Much as I respect what they do at the sanctuary, to be honest, I'm here asking for a favor."

"To foster mustangs on their way to the prison system, right? Sounds like a win-win to me." She started up the stairs again. "You're looking out for the animals instead of looking for profit. That equals no charge. Don't argue."

Lucas chuckled. "How much sway do you have with Melanie and Shea? I could use someone like you on my side."

"Surely they aren't giving you a hard time." She stopped on the second floor, her eyes narrowing. "Well, not Shea—she's in California. I can't imagine Melanie opposing the idea."

"No, she doesn't, but it's not her decision alone."

"Do they have to put it to a vote?" Rachel frowned. "I guess the board will have to approve it, but that seems silly." She shook her head. "It's not a real board. It's more…" She pressed her lips together, looking as if she regretted saying too much. "My brother Jesse is involved. He's out in the barn but maybe you two can talk later."

"I was hoping either he or Trace might be around."

Rachel continued down the long hall but he didn't miss her smile. "So I see you and Mel had some time to chat."

"We did," he said, carefully sticking to business. "She mentioned your brothers were involved in the gathers."

"Usually, yes, though they'll stand down if they feel

the government is jumping the gun and the herd doesn't need thinning to survive." She stopped at a door almost at the end. "The guest wing is on the other side of the house. These rooms belong to my family. It'll be quieter here, and if you want to stay longer than one night, no problem."

"I don't want to put you out. I'm fine with being a paying guest."

"You're not putting anyone out. Unless you'd rather stay on the floor with the women." She met his eyes, her lips twitching, probably from seeing the dread on his face. "That's what I thought." She opened the door. "It's a bit small, but the bed's a queen and the bathroom across the hall is all yours. Everyone else has their own."

He entered the room, noticed the pair of oak nightstands and huge matching dresser. And still there was plenty of space to move around. The room was far from small. But then, he'd lived in a six-by-eight cell for three years.

"I'll leave you to get settled. When you come downstairs, the kitchen is on the left. Someone's usually in there, but if not, help yourself to the fridge."

"Rachel?"

She turned back to him with a smile, her brows arched expectantly. She was pretty, probably about Melanie's age. He would bet they'd gone to school together.

"Thanks," he said, the inadequate word feeling thick on his tongue, guilt smoldering in his gut. Would she have welcomed him had she known he'd been incarcerated until a year ago? "I appreciate this."

"Oh, please. It's no trouble. Come down soon, and I'll tell Jesse you're here. Poor guy doesn't know what to do with himself with Shea gone."

Lucas stared at the door long after she'd pulled it closed behind her. This wasn't like him, to start getting itchy about the past. Have misgivings over whether he was doing the right thing inching his way back into society as if he were just like everyone else. He'd paid his debt, served every last minute of his sentence. There'd been no time off for good behavior. Cal Jessup, his powerful and wily neighbor, had seen to that.

The ruthless bastard had taken the stand and crafted the perfect statement of how he'd feared for his life. And he'd paid his hired man to swear to it. The memory of that ill-fated October afternoon was burned in Lucas's mind forever. But for his own sanity, and any hope of having a decent life, he'd learned to step away from those thoughts as soon as they came up.

His bag was light, considering it held most of his personal belongings. He unzipped it, pulled out a clean pair of jeans, his toiletries and a collared shirt to hang in the closet. The three extra T-shirts, he left rolled up in the bag.

Hell, he knew why he was edgy. He hadn't been around people like Melanie and Rachel since being released. Normal, hardworking folks who were warm and open, inviting him into their safe, comfortable lives. Giving him free rein and trusting that when he moved on, he'd leave everything and everyone just as he'd found them. No, it was more an assumption than trust on their part. They didn't know he was an ex-con and had no reason to worry.

In theory, keeping his past private had been an easy decision to make. Much as he believed in Prison Reform Now, he had no intention of becoming the poster boy for the organization. Mostly he crossed paths with two kinds of people: the well-bred women who ran PRN and the government lackeys who facilitated moving the horses from the wild to the prisons.

The women all knew about him because they'd plucked him fresh out of the penal system. Lucas wasn't stupid. He figured half of them got off imagining him as dangerous, untamed, a man struggling between good and evil. Entertaining the possibility he could be seduced by the dark side excited them. Some of the ladies weren't much different from prison pen pals, except they had money.

But nice small-town women like Melanie... He didn't meet her kind anymore. Even though he'd almost married one....

Out of habit, he quickly shut down all thoughts of Peggy. He inhaled deeply, feeling relief flow through him. Thankfully, the fleeting image of her oval face and golden hair no longer packed the same punch it once had. Neither did the resentment or the desire for revenge. Every day, it was getting better, or at least easier. According to the shrinks, he'd be adjusted to life on the outside in no time.

Yeah, he'd consider listening to their one-size-fits-all conclusions after they'd been unjustly locked in a cage for three years.

The thing was, they hadn't been wrong. Not about him. He had done well, using his time productively and rarely dwelling on the lost years and thoughts of revenge or mistaking violence for a solution. He'd gone inside a decent, hardworking rancher, but he could've come out a completely different man. The first year had been pure hell. Angry and bitter, he'd looked for trouble around every corner. But it was the Wild Horse Training Program that had pulled him back on track, not some shrink.

After a quick shower, Lucas went downstairs, hoping he hadn't missed Jesse. He heard the clank of pool balls, skipped the kitchen and followed the sound. Rachel's sudden burst of laughter coming from the den made him smile. She had one of those infectious personalities.

Clutching a pair of empty longneck bottles, she saw him in the doorway. "Hey, here he is. Lucas, this is Jesse and Matt," she said, gesturing for him to join them.

The taller dark-haired guy with the military cut rested his cue stick against the wall. "I'm Jesse," he said, extending his hand, his expression welcoming.

"Good timing, Lucas." The other man, who obviously was Matt, exchanged his stick for a beer and shook Lucas's hand. "I'm tired of getting whipped."

Rachel bumped him with her hip. "You better not let Trace hear you say that. He'll never let you live it down. Lucas, food, beer, soda—what can I get you?"

He settled for a bottle of Coors, turned down a cue stick and watched while Jesse finished running the table.

Matt muttered a mild oath and shook his head. "Why do I put myself through this?"

Jesse grinned. "For what it's worth, you're improving."

Keeping a smile in check, Rachel made a sympathetic sound as she took Matt's hand and led him away from the pool table.

They sat on the overstuffed couch in front of a massive stone fireplace. Jesse and Lucas each took a club chair, facing them.

"What do you think of the changes they've made out at Safe Haven?" Rachel asked. "Impressive, huh?"

"To tell you the truth, this is my first time out here. I've been working for PRN—that's Prison Reform Now—for about a year. We heard about the sanctuary when they had to move a herd of mustangs and strays."

"Yeah, Blackfoot Falls is pretty much out of the way," Jesse said. "Initially I thought it was a strange move to open the place this far north, but they've had their hands full from the get-go. A lot of animals have been turned away. Not enough hay or grain to feed them."

"I heard you fly animal rescue."

Jesse shrugged. "Only when they need me." The straight line of his back, the clean-shaven jaw...definitely military. "A co-op group owns the plane and a chopper. Safe Haven isn't a member but I try to help them out when I can."

"What about the Bureau of Land Management? Melanie mentioned you help with the roundups."

Jesse snorted, his laid-back expression disappearing. "The BLM and I don't always see eye to eye. But hey, I don't hold it against the guys working the gathers. They're government employees doing their job. Hell, I did that for eight years myself."

"Air Force?" Lucas asked.

Jesse nodded. "You?"

"Nope." Lucas cursed his own stupidity. The last thing he wanted was to talk about himself, but he'd opened the door. "Thought about it, but I'm the only son. Someone had to keep the ranch going."

"Tell us about your organization," Rachel suggested. She was curled up against Matt, who had his hand on her leg. "You were looking for allies. Jesse has some influence with Shea."

"Yeah." Jesse coughed on his mouthful of beer. "Not much."

Rachel shook her head. "My poor brother, so smart and so dumb at the same time."

"You guys must've all gone to school together, huh? The three of you and Melanie..." Lucas let his words trail off, hoping like hell he hadn't sounded obvious. Tricky business getting information without giving any.

"We're different ages," Rachel said, "but we all grew up here, so we know each other. Not Shea, though. She moved here the beginning of the year from California."

Lucas gave up getting any info about Melanie. He just nodded and took another gulp of beer. Better just stick to the reason he was here. "Rachel, you obviously have a basic understanding of the Wild Horse Training Program." He glanced at the two men. "What about you?"

"I've heard of it," Jesse said with a slight frown, as if searching his memory. "It's big in Wyoming and Colorado, if I'm not mistaken."

"And Nevada," Lucas added. "They have half of the

country's wild horse and burro population, so they're happy to turn stock from the gathers over to the prison farms."

"So, what?" Matt jumped in. "They don't want to send them out of state?"

"Too much red tape and money," Rachel said. "The state doesn't want the extra headache."

Everyone looked at her in surprise.

"What?" She shrugged. "I only know because Melanie told me. She called after you left." Rachel looked at Lucas. "We chatted a bit. She's excited about the program. She likes knowing where the horses they foster end up."

Lucas knew Melanie was in favor of the program. He shouldn't have been surprised she'd discussed it with Rachel.

"Why didn't Melanie come over?" Matt asked. "It's Friday night. No school tomorrow." He nudged Rachel. "Call her."

Rachel and Jesse exchanged startled glances. They seemed to know something Matt didn't.

"She won't come." Rachel shook her head. "I'm sure she's busy."

"It's the weekend." Matt frowned at Rachel as if he thought she was being unreasonable. He must've seen something in her face that told him to drop it, because he settled back and turned to Lucas. "So you want to use Safe Haven as a way station."

Lucas had lost his train of thought. He wasn't even sure if he'd heard Matt correctly. Taking a shot in the dark, he nodded. His thoughts had strayed to Melanie and the puzzled look Rachel and her brother had given each other. Maybe Lucas wasn't the only one holding on to a secret.

MELANIE ARRIVED AT Safe Haven earlier than usual on Saturday. She'd tried to convince herself it made more sense to take care of her church duties first, but she didn't know when to expect Lucas. They hadn't set a time. Foolish on her part, but she'd been too flustered for that sort of logic. To think she'd actually hoped he would kiss her again after they'd returned to the stable. Kathy and Levi had left, but Nina and her boyfriend had been right there in the barn.

That was all Melanie needed…to have Nina catch them kissing. She was a reliable volunteer, given she was only nineteen, but she wasn't known for her discretion. And nosy? Oh, yes, she'd pummeled Melanie with a dozen questions before Lucas had driven out of the parking lot.

Covering a yawn, she opened the unlocked door to the office and headed straight for the coffeemaker. Once she'd gotten the brew started, she turned to the volunteer board she had yet to hang. Her heart sank. Nina was scheduled for tonight again. How had Melanie not remembered? That meant the cabin wouldn't be free for Lucas. And she already knew the Sundance was booked.

She heard a vehicle coming down the drive and glanced out the window. Something about seeing Lucas's truck triggered a memory. A dream. From last night. Lucas. Her. A meadow of wildflowers…

Another remembered fragment brought a warm flush to her chest and up her neck. Lucas…naked…aroused… the sunlight bathing his glistening bronzed skin.

Oh, dear God. *Now* she had to remember?

She hurried away from the window, resorting to thoughts of vacuuming—her most dreaded chore—but the stubborn image of Lucas's naked body stuck to her brain like superglue. She grabbed a file off the desk and fanned herself, willing the blotchy red skin to disappear before he found her.

It was useless. Being magically transported to Antarctica was her only hope of cooling off. So, yeah, she was screwed. At least he wouldn't know the embarrassing reason why she was glowing like an overripe tomato. She could lie about having a rare disease. He'd get back in his truck, and that would be that.

She heard the knock, thought briefly about not answering, then decided that would be childish. Besides, her car was in plain view. She sank into the chair behind the desk. "It's unlocked."

Lucas opened the door and walked in with a killer smile on his handsome face. "Good morning."

"It'll be much better after the coffee is ready."

"Ah." He held up a white paper bag. "Maybe this will help. Rachel sent poppy-seed muffins fresh out of the oven."

"Who made them?"

"Hilda."

"Oh, good."

"And if I'd said Rachel?"

Melanie pressed her lips together but couldn't keep from laughing. "I'd plead the Fifth."

He set the bag in front of her. "I'll keep that to myself."

"Thank you." She couldn't keep staring into his blue eyes or waiting for the smile tugging at his mouth. If she did, she might remember more of the dream.

At the thought, she shot out of the chair. Of course, it was too late. In her mind's eye, he was gloriously naked. She knew for sure that his chest was smooth and muscled, no imagination required. And the rest of him…

She doubted her skin had returned to normal yet, and she could feel another wave of heat warming her chest and face. Great time for her to be wearing a scooped-neck shirt. Just great.

He'd moved back, clearly startled at her sudden leap toward the coffeemaker. "I could've poured you a cup."

"Oh, that's okay. I put stuff in it." In truth, she wasn't quite so anxious to add more caffeine to the mix of nerves and embarrassment fueling her ridiculous mania. Earlier she'd plowed through half a pot to combat the restless night she'd spent battling her pillow.

She turned over a pair of orange mugs sitting at the ready, then drummed her fingers on the filing cabinet they used as a counter while she waited for the last of the coffee to drip.

"I'm sorry," he murmured.

With a cautious look over her shoulder, she saw that he'd put some distance between them. "For what?"

"I shouldn't have kissed you."

Her stomach lurched, but she managed a small laugh. "Did I miss something?"

"Last night." Lucas shook his head with clear self-disgust. "You're jumpy. It's my fault."

"No. You're wrong," she said, turning to face him. "I haven't given it a thought." She noticed his gaze briefly sweep the flushed skin along her neckline, and she sighed. "It's not as painful as it looks."

His lashes didn't so much as flicker. Regret had replaced any trace of his earlier amusement. He seemed tense, his shoulders pulled back and stiff.

"Okay, look, I fibbed. I did think about the kiss." She fisted her hands until her nails dug into her palms. "A lot. But only because I liked it. I wanted you to kiss me. If you knew how long I'd been trying to work up the courage to kiss you first, you'd laugh."

He stared back, his brows slightly puckered as if he was trying to make sense of her admission. Or perhaps he couldn't decide if she was lying. Or if he should escape while he still could.

The silence became too much. "If you don't say something soon—" she swallowed "—I'll get *really* flustered, and that *will* be your fault."

His somber expression eased. So did the tension in

his shoulders. For a moment the faint glimmer of a smile reached his eyes. He moved closer, and she relaxed her fists. "Are you going to share that coffee?"

"That's it?" Melanie laughed a little. "That's all you have to say?"

"For now." He reached around her for the carafe, his eyes staying on her face.

She supposed it would've been polite to give him room, but she couldn't make herself move. She could feel his heat, smell the fresh scent of his recent shower. Lifting her mouth for a kiss wouldn't come as a shock to him after her confession.

Melanie had barely tilted her head when he cupped her chin.

6

She was brave. Lucas knew it had taken a lot for her to admit she'd wanted him to kiss her last night. Braver still for offering her mouth to him. But that sexy look in her pretty brown eyes? She was looking for trouble. Extending an invitation he doubted she was ready to follow through on.

Holding her chin steady, he brushed his thumb across her soft bottom lip. It quivered, just a little, just enough to rekindle the lust he'd spent half the night trying to ignore. What was it about her that drew him? She was shy about certain things, sweet and completely without guile. In some ways she reminded him of Peggy, but this feeling growing inside had nothing to do with his ex-fiancée.

Maybe he was tired of the pushy women who'd been too eager to jump in his bed. At first, after he'd done without for three years, it had been great having his pick of every shape, size and flavor. He'd had no complaints. But after a while, all those meaningless encounters did was feed the emptiness in his soul.

Melanie's lids fluttered closed, and he studied her thick lashes, her small nose, the outline of her pretty bow-shaped lips. Just as he lowered his mouth for a taste, there was a thump at the door.

They were quick to break apart.

Lucas lifted the carafe, while Melanie reached for a mug and said, “It’s open.”

Levi entered carrying a to-go cup and a carton of cream. “Mornin’, Mel. I was hoping you had coffee made.” He nodded at Lucas. “How’s your back, son? You did most of the unloading yesterday.”

“I’m good. When I was a kid, my stepfather liked telling everyone I was strong as an ox.”

“You’re still strong.” Levi chuckled. “I saw your truck in the lot and told Kathy I had a mind to go pick up another load of logs and feed while we still had your help.”

“Feel free.” Lucas shrugged. “No need to rush, though. I’ll be around for a while.” From his peripheral vision he saw Melanie jerk a look at him.

Even Levi seemed to notice her jumpy reaction. He shifted his weight from one foot to the other. “If I could get topped off,” he muttered, holding up his cup, “I’ll get started in the quarantine stable.”

“Sure.” Melanie gestured for him to help himself, then moved to the desk and pulled out a drawer. “How much for the cream?”

“Don’t worry about it,” Levi said, waving her off.

“Darn it, Levi. Don’t get stubborn on me. That’s what petty cash is for. Sadly, I know what a teacher’s pension amounts to. Take the money.”

Levi glared at the folded bills she held out to him, then at her. “You used to be such a sweet, obedient girl. Always minding your elders. What happened?”

She came around the desk and stuffed the money in his shirt pocket. “I grew up.”

“I was just teasing,” Levi said cheerfully. “You’re still a sweet girl, Mel. Did she mention I was her high school teacher?”

Lucas shook his head, surprised she seemed annoyed. Maybe she didn't like being called "sweet."

"Yep, you ask any teacher who had Melanie. They'd all tell you the same thing. Smart as a whip, always behaved like a little lady, the model student—"

"All right, that's enough." She held up a hand to Levi. "Or you'll see quite another side of me."

The man chuckled as if he didn't believe that for a second. He finished stirring his coffee, then pressed the top back on the travel cup.

She sighed. "You might want to reconsider picking up another load of supplies today," she said, then turned to Lucas. "The cabin isn't available tonight after all. I didn't realize Nina would still be using it."

"No problem. Rachel is letting me stay." He would've preferred the cabin or sleeping outside, but he wasn't picky.

"How? The Sundance is booked solid. Rachel told me herself."

"She took pity on me. I have a room in the main house."

"Oh. So you wouldn't have to..." She grinned. "That was nice of her."

"Very nice. Except we're having a disagreement over payment. She won't accept any money because, as she puts it, I'm 'a friend of Safe Haven.'"

"Well, you are, aren't you?" Levi had stopped at the door to listen.

"I pay my own way," he said and meant it. "I won't feel comfortable staying there for free." He met Melanie's eyes. "I'm counting on you to back me up."

"I'll call Rachel," she said, breathing in deep and looking away. "Can't promise it'll do any good."

Levi eyed them with a faint speculative frown, then opened the door. "Well, I'd better get to work before Kathy comes looking for me."

"We'll be out right after I make the call," Melanie said, casting him a brief glance.

"You can talk to Rachel in person." Lucas picked up a mug. "She's invited us to supper tonight."

Melanie blinked at him. "Tonight? Both of us?"

Apparently Levi had forgotten he'd been about to leave. Shamelessly eavesdropping, he waited in the open doorway.

She slowly shook her head. "It's Saturday—"

Lucas noted the color blooming in her cheeks. "You already have a date?"

"A what?" She let out a laugh. "No. No. It's just that I'm always busy on the weekends. Rachel understands."

"Take the night off, Melanie," Levi said quietly. "Go to the Sundance. The McAllisters are such nice folks."

"Yes, of course they are, but that doesn't change the fact that I have a lot to do." She was getting defensive, crossing her arms over her chest.

After the look Rachel and Jesse had exchanged last night, Lucas should've foreseen this, maybe mentioned dinner in private. Damn, he really wanted to spend the evening with her. "Hey, you know what? No big deal. It'll probably be noisy and crowded. They're expecting a bunch of new guests."

She frowned, her lips pursing into a slight pout. "Right. Saturday is usually a big check-in day."

He heard the door close. So did she, because they both glanced in that direction. Levi had finally left.

Lucas silently cursed his stupidity. He'd seen how she'd gotten nervous when Levi had joined them. "Should I not have mentioned supper in front of Levi?"

"It's fine." She sighed, gazing toward the window, her thoughts obviously drifting. "Maybe I can swing dinner if I hurry and get my act together. I have a huge list of things to do."

"I can help." He spread his arms. "Use me."

Her lips parted, she stared at him for a long drawn-out moment. And then she just laughed.

"What's so funny?"

"Nothing." She shook her head, averted her eyes. She glanced at him again, her gaze roaming across his chest before she looked up and caught him staring back. "Nothing," she repeated, this time more adamantly.

"All right." He didn't believe her, but he didn't want to piss her off or give her another reason to blow off dinner. "Put me to work," he said, wondering if tonight he'd find out if the sweet, pretty schoolteacher was still looking for trouble.

MELANIE'S GRIP ON the rake handle tightened as she watched Lucas pick up a bale of hay and hoist it to his shoulder, causing the snug brown T-shirt to stretch across his back. His muscles were getting quite the workout, even the ones in his butt, and for the first time she completely understood the term *eye candy.* When he'd offered to help Levi and Chuck rearrange the barn to make room for the last cutting of hay, she'd assumed he'd make use of the borrowed Bobcat. Not lug around the huge bales by himself.

And instead of finishing her share of the barn chores, what was she doing? Standing around and staring like a love-struck schoolgirl. Her only consolation was that Kathy and Liberty had been eyeing him, too. Though Liberty was only fifteen.

Kathy stopped sweeping to blot her face with the red bandanna she wore tied loosely around her neck. "I must say, that cowboy sure knows how to fill out a pair of jeans."

"He's young enough to be your son," Liberty said, grinning when Kathy turned to glare at her.

"In case you haven't noticed, I'm not dead." Kathy

sniffed. "A woman at any age can still appreciate a fine-looking man."

"What's that?" Levi had come up behind them. Judging by his expression, he truly hadn't heard. Not that he would've minded his wife's remark.

"Why, nothing worth repeating." Kathy smiled at him, then gave the mischievous Liberty a warning look. "Guess I'll go muck out the stable. Liberty, why don't you come help?"

That wiped the smirk off the girl's face, and Melanie couldn't help laughing. Liberty might want to argue but she didn't dare put up a fuss. Considering trouble followed her around like an eager puppy, the girl took her duties seriously. But mucking out stalls was her most dreaded chore. Not that she had a choice. Volunteering at Safe Haven was court-appointed community service.

She sent Melanie a pleading look. "Really? Is that what you want me to do next?"

"It has to be done," she said, pulling off a work glove to take care of an itch at the back of her neck. "But if you really don't want to do it, I'm sure Kathy can manage by herself."

Liberty's smug expression lasted only the second it took her to glance at Kathy, who played her role perfectly. She was talking to Levi while absently pressing a hand to her lower back, right where it sometimes stiffened on her.

The girl bit her lip. "No," she said, turning back to Melanie. "I'll do it. Maybe there's something else Kathy could do. Collect eggs, maybe?"

A warm sense of satisfaction pooled inside Melanie. She and Kathy knew Liberty wasn't a bad kid. Sure, she'd had a number of scrapes with the sheriff's department, but she also had little to no parental supervision. She had a good heart and they were hopeful that between Liberty's involvement with the sanctuary and her aunt moving to Blackfoot Falls to look after her, the teenager would straighten out.

Kathy glanced over her shoulder. "Come on, kiddo. Let's go clean out those stalls."

"I can do it by myself." Liberty gave her a shrug. "Find something else to do."

"No, we'll do it together. I have to work the stiffness out of my old bones." Kathy gave Melanie a private wink.

She watched them head out, then swung her gaze toward Lucas. Levi had stopped him on his way to pick up another bale.

Her cell buzzed and she checked the caller ID, though she didn't know why she bothered. Gertrude made the same call every Saturday morning. "Hello, Mrs. Wagner. No, I haven't forgotten that I need to do your shopping this afternoon."

The elderly woman snorted. "Well, now, if you'd keep your panties on for a minute, I'll tell you why I called. It's my kitchen sink. Something got it all stopped up."

"Okay," Melanie said slowly, her mind racing ahead. The problem would likely be fixed with a plunger, so that wouldn't throw her off schedule. "I'll have a look at it when I bring your groceries."

"It can't wait that long."

"I'll be there in three hours." She glanced at her watch, then saw Levi and Lucas walking toward her. "Can't you use your bathroom sink for now?"

"Sorry, dear, I can't do that." Her sudden conciliatory tone did not bode well.

Melanie sighed. "Tell me you haven't been cooking again."

Levi heard and was shaking his head. He knew exactly who she was talking to. A faint smile lifted Lucas's lips, making her wonder if she'd rolled her eyes.

"Mrs. Wagner? Are you there?"

The woman responded with a wheezing cough. That meant one of two things: she'd been sneaking cigarettes again, or she didn't want to answer. "I might also have a small leak," she said.

"You might— Is the floor wet?"

"Yes, I believe it's a bit damp."

Melanie rubbed her tired eyes. Translation…there was a puddle. "I'll be right there."

"Will you be able to fix it, dear?"

"I don't know anything about plumbing…." So much for dinner at the Sundance with Lucas. "I'll find someone who does. Just please, stay out of the kitchen so you don't slip."

After securing the woman's promise, Melanie disconnected the call.

"If she's been cooking, she's tried to hide the evidence," Levi said.

"I know." She pocketed the phone. "I'm sorry to bail on you," she said, looking from Levi to Lucas. She was even sorrier that now she'd probably miss dinner, but she wouldn't tell Lucas yet.

"There's not much left. Can you and Chuck finish up?" Lucas asked Levi, who nodded. "I'll go with you."

"Me?" Melanie felt like an idiot. Who else? He was looking right at her. "No, I'll be fine."

"Look, I know enough about plumbing to fix a leak."

Thoughts were swirling and colliding inside her head. Levi was giving her a puzzled look. It wasn't that she minded the help; she just hadn't decided how much she wanted Lucas knowing about her.

"It's the start of hunting season," Levi reminded her. "You might not find anyone else if it turns out the leak is bad."

Lucas hadn't waited for her to give him the green light. He'd already yanked off his gloves and pulled a cloth out of his back pocket to mop his face. "Let's take my truck. I have a tool chest in the back."

"You don't have to do this," she protested.

"You're right. Let's go." He cupped her elbow but then immediately lowered his hand.

She wasn't sure if it was because Levi was watching them. "We'll be back as soon as possible," she told him, already backing out of the barn.

Levi waved her off. "You get the rest of your Saturday chores done. Can't have you using them as an excuse to miss supper."

With an exasperated toss of her head, she turned around and caught Lucas's expression of amusement. "What?"

He slid her a glance but said nothing.

"Is that why you offered to go with me?"

"That's one reason."

"I'm not looking for excuses to bow out. Weekends are busy. If I didn't want to go tonight, I would've told you."

"You need anything from the office?" He veered toward his truck.

"I should probably take my car so you won't have to make the trip out here again. Plus, I have other errands to run."

"We'll do them together."

She smiled. He didn't understand, and she still wasn't sure she wanted him to see her in her element. Most of her Saturdays revolved around helping members of her father's congregation. Everyone seemed to think she was a darn saint. There were worse things to be labeled. It probably shouldn't annoy her, but it did.

"Ride with me."

Only after he spoke did she realize she'd stopped walking, her gaze idly fixed on his dented bumper. The damage was her fault. She still felt awful about the accident.

"I wonder if there's someone at the gas station who could look at that dent."

"Not today."

"How do you know?" She turned to him, unprepared for the dazzling effect of his blue eyes in direct sunlight. "Did you stop in town?"

He squinted against the glare. "The truck's not a priority." He moved his hand, and she held her breath, expecting him to touch her. But he only rubbed the back of his neck. "What's wrong, Melanie? Afraid to be seen with me in town?"

"Why would you say such a…?" Had Levi or Chuck mentioned she was Pastor Ray's daughter? So what if they had? This wasn't high school. Lucas wouldn't ditch her. As for Mrs. Wagner and the other elderly ladies on her list, it was almost a given they'd say something embarrassing about her. "Here's the thing—if I ride with you and you get bored, you can't leave me stranded in town without my car. So you'd better think twice about…"

She trailed off, amazed that he'd so rudely walked away. If he'd changed his mind, fine. But he could've at least let her finish.

He opened the truck's passenger door, moved something off the seat, then stood back waiting for her. His expression was blank, except he still managed to communicate his complete ease, which oddly made her nervous. That and the way the T-shirt clung to his chest and shoulder muscles, reminding her of how he looked bare chested.

Melanie took a deep involuntary breath and forced herself to move. No need to feel like a lamb being led to slaughter. "Okay," she said, finding a foothold on the step-up. "But I warned you."

His warm calloused palm cupped her elbow until she was seated. "Noted."

Her skin tingled from the casual touch, even after he'd

let her go, and continued to do so while he rounded the hood, then slid behind the steering wheel. She rubbed her arm, trying to stop the sensation. It was ridiculous for a twenty-seven-year-old woman to be feeling this way.

She eyed his Stetson sitting on the console between them and wondered why he hadn't worn it. He'd look good. Oh, Lord, he looked good now.

Lucas turned the key he'd left in the ignition and the engine purred to life. "Where are we headed?"

"To town."

After checking the mirror, he slid his arm along the seat behind her shoulders and looked out the rear window as he reversed. "You seem tense."

"Me?" She shook her head, then nodded. "I'm a little tense."

"Does it have anything to do with me?"

"I want to go to dinner tonight. I really do. But I have a lot of things on my list."

"So you said." He tried to control a smile, but she saw it tugging at his mouth.

"Do I amuse you, Mr. Sloan?"

His right eyebrow went up. "You do a lot of things to me, Ms. Knowles," he said, shifting gears and giving her a look that could melt a pound of butter.

The tingling started again. "Are you flirting with me?" she asked, surprised at how easy it was to give it back to him.

"Damn straight."

Melanie laughed. "I know you're teasing, but you can't do that in front of Mrs. Wagner. She won't understand."

He frowned at her, his expression more curious than anything. "Who said I'm teasing?"

Not knowing how to answer, she stared at the road ahead. "You have to veer right to get to Blackfoot Falls."

After a stretch of unnerving silence, she glanced at him. "You know how small towns are."

For a moment the only sound in the cab was the air conditioner whirring to beat out the September heat. "Where do you live?"

"In town."

"By yourself?"

"Yes." She'd bet he assumed she still lived with her parents. Seven months ago he wouldn't have been wrong. And then she'd had her big aha moment. She loved her mother, but Melanie didn't want to be an extension of her. And that was exactly how everyone seemed to view her. "I'm in a small two-bedroom house. It's convenient, close to school, not too far from Safe Haven. Why are you smiling like that?"

"You don't have to justify where you choose to live."

She started to object, but he was right. She realized that after explaining repeatedly why she'd left her parents' home, her defensive tone had practically become engrained. "You might be the only person in Montana who has that opinion."

Lucas smiled. "If I were to ask about you in town, what would people tell me about Melanie Knowles?"

Her sigh turned into a groan. "I have a bad feeling you're about to find out."

7

"YOU SURE TOOK your sweet time getting here," Mrs. Wagner said before she'd completely opened the front door. She cut short her sniff of disapproval the second she saw Lucas. "Who are you?" she asked, leaning on her walker and peering at him through her thick glasses.

"Do not be crabby with me," Melanie said, even though the woman hadn't spared her a glance. "You've been cooking. I can smell it."

The acrid tang of smoke was in the air, all right. Lucas figured it wouldn't be a bad thing to leave the door open and crank up a few windows. But the tiny elderly woman with the short snow-white hair hadn't moved. She continued to stare at him and block their entrance.

"This is Lucas Sloan. He's going to look at your sink. Now, may we come in?"

"I'm Gertrude," she said, lowering her chin to take another look at him over her wire rims.

"Morning, ma'am." He smiled and finished scraping the bottom of his boots on the upside-down welcome mat.

Curiosity lit a gleam in her faded blue eyes. "My, but you're a handsome buck. Where did you come from?"

Melanie let out a short laugh. "Mrs. Wagner, do you

want Lucas to think we have no manners here in Blackfoot Falls?"

"You think I care what anyone thinks? At my age, a body doesn't have that kind of time to waste." She cautiously stepped back, slowly moving the walker with her. Then, pausing, she frowned at Melanie. "Don't you go calling my son to tattle. Dropping a slice of bread in a toaster ain't cooking."

As soon as she maneuvered the walker around, he and Melanie exchanged smiles. That wasn't burned toast. Smelled more like overfried fish.

They stepped inside the small cluttered house with its garish blue walls, and Lucas closed the door behind them. "We should open a few windows," he said, leaning close to Melanie so only she would hear.

She let out a little sigh of exasperation that carried her warm breath to the side of his neck. "Yes, but only the ones with screens or we'll have a hundred flies in here."

He studied the column of her slender throat down to her dainty collarbones visible just above her neckline. With her small pointed chin and wrists so tiny he could hold them both in one hand, she really was delicately put together. He couldn't recall ever thinking of a woman in those terms. "I'll go check the leak, then get my tools," he muttered before he did something foolish.

"What are you two whispering about?" From over her shoulder, Gertrude frowned at them.

"We're going to open some windows, Mrs. Wagner," Melanie said. "Just for a little bit."

"And let all that heat in?"

"It's not that warm outside," Melanie said and rolled her eyes at Lucas.

He held back a grin. "I'm following you, Mrs. Wagner, so you can show me the problem."

"Call me Gertrude." She gave him a once-over. "Or

Gerdie," she said, her wide smile displaying overly large dentures. With a little more spring in her step, she resumed pushing the walker toward the kitchen.

All he did was look at Melanie, and she hastily covered her mouth. "Do not make me laugh," she mumbled. "I mean it." She lowered her hand to shoo him. "Go."

He watched her hurry to a window and struggle to lift it. Much as he wanted to help, he didn't dare. Damn, but he'd never been turned on by a pair of collarbones and a giddy laugh before. With a mental shake, he went after Gertrude. The powerful burned smell led him directly to the dingy yellow kitchen. The tulip wallpaper was old and faded, and he could see where someone had tried to mend the cracks in the tan linoleum floor.

It still wasn't safe for a woman relying on a walker. He could see places where the wheel might get caught. On the drive Melanie had given him the scoop on the elderly lady, whose age was somewhere between eighty-one and eighty-five. Gertrude had outlived two husbands and a daughter, was still sharp and stubborn as a mule and refused to move to Billings to live with her only son and his family. She'd grown up in this house and given birth to both her children in the same bedroom where she herself had been brought into the world. Gertrude Wagner wasn't going anywhere. Not until they carried her body out on a gurney.

He stood in the doorway and watched her carefully skirt one of the worrisome cracks. "Better stay where you are," he told her. "I can see where the floor is wet."

She edged back. "The water is coming from underneath," she said, leaning forward to peer into the sink. "It's gone down some. An hour ago the backup dang near made it to the top."

Using the toe of his boot, he pushed aside a pile of soggy rags so he could open the lower cabinet door. "Did you stuff something down the drain you shouldn't have?"

She sniffed. "I know better than to do that."

"You're not supposed to be frying fish, either." He looked over at her and watched her initial outrage fade to sheepishness. "I'm not trying to embarrass you, Gertrude. Just like Melanie isn't being mean when she tells you to leave the cooking to her. It's for your own safety."

"I'm not an invalid," she muttered and tightened her mouth.

He crouched down to check the pipe. "No, but I heard you've had a couple mishaps this year. Melanie worries about you." He stuck his head in as far as he could. The pipe was old. He could fix the leak, but the repair would be temporary. Replacing everything was the right thing to do. He'd have to discuss it with Melanie first.

"No one needs to worry about me. Been taking care of myself since before my second husband passed," she said with a huff. "Henry spent his last year abed, and I took care of him, too."

"Yep, everyone needs help from time to time." He pushed to his feet. "That's why Melanie looks after you."

Normally, it wasn't his style to butt into another person's affairs, and this feeling of protectiveness toward Melanie… He wasn't sure where that was coming from, either. But he knew she was concerned about the woman, and for good reason. Trouble was, everyone seemed willing to let Gertrude delude herself, even at the risk of her own safety. She needed to pay attention to the boundaries her son and Melanie had set.

"I'm going out to my truck for some tools." He found a clean rag to wipe his hands, then finally looked at Gertrude again, meeting her intensely curious eyes.

"Where are you from, Lucas? How do you know our Melanie?"

"Wyoming. Safe Haven."

Gertrude snorted a laugh. "You're a man of few words when the shoe's on the other foot."

He smiled. "Melanie worries. I doubt you want that for her."

"No," she agreed, sighing and leaning heavily on the walker. "The girl doesn't have a mean bone in her body. She'd rather tiptoe around my stubborn pride than point it out. Truth be told, only reason I get to stay in this house is because of her. But then, Melanie's a damn saint. Ask anyone."

Lucas had to laugh at that. Gertrude didn't appear to see the irony of using those two words together. "How about you sit for a spell?" He pulled out a battered oak chair from the kitchen table. The set was old but sturdy. "You can supervise me."

She studied him with shrewd eyes, then let out a rusty chuckle. "Lord, I'll have to go easy on the poor girl. She's got her hands full with you." Gertrude took her time getting to the chair and then wearily sank down. "Go on. I'll be right here when you get back."

"Yes, ma'am." He pulled the walker out of her reach, and she gave him a cranky look.

Lucas just grinned. When he turned, he saw Melanie standing in the doorway watching them. Baffled by her sullen expression, he motioned for her to follow him outside. She couldn't have overheard anything objectionable. Yet she looked as if she wanted to throw something.

MELANIE WAITED FOR HIM on the porch. If he dared to call her Saint Melanie he could go to dinner by himself tonight. Of all the names she'd ever been called, she hated that one the most. But of course someone at some point today would have to pull out the moniker and dust it off.

In the back of her mind she'd known it might happen if she brought Lucas with her. But within minutes of arriving in town? Jeez. All she needed now was for Mrs. Wagner to tell him how Melanie had followed in her sainted mother's footsteps. Nothing to excite a man like being with the town martyr.

It was no surprise that two of Mrs. Wagner's neighbors were peeking out from their kitchen windows. They didn't recognize Lucas's truck. She waved to Celeste Lindstrom, who waved back. Lillian Brown, the biggest gossip on the street, pretended she hadn't been pressing her nose to the glass and slowly let the ruffled green curtain fall back into place.

Oh, let them talk.... She didn't care. In fact, it was time she had a new image, so good.

"She needs a new elbow pipe," Lucas said behind her. "I can fix this one temporarily, at least unclog the P-trap, but it'll be leaking again in a month."

"Oh." She sighed. "Well, that is a problem."

"Does the local hardware store stock plumbing supplies? It's a common pipe. I can pick one up and do the job right now."

"I honestly don't know what Mr. Jorgensen carries along that line." She stared at the rag in his hand. He had some scars near his knuckles that she hadn't noticed before. "I didn't expect this to be a big deal. You shouldn't be wasting your time—"

"Relax, Melanie." He touched her arm, then let the tips of his fingers trail down to her wrist. "I don't mind helping."

She moved her arm away and glanced over to see if Lillian was still at the window. "Only if I can pay you."

"Pay me?" Lucas cursed under his breath, but she heard.

Startled, she turned to meet his gaze.

"Now, *that* really pisses me off." He wasn't kidding. He did not look happy.

"I'm sorry. I meant no offense."

With an almost-imperceptible shake of his head, he stared past her toward the mountains, his expression dark and brooding like yesterday. He reminded her of Heathcliff on the moors. Mysterious and changeable. Cool, detached, his eyes distant, he seemed nothing like the man who'd changed the bus tire and kept Mrs. Wagner out of harm's way.

The silence… She couldn't stand it anymore. "Lucas?"

Rubbing a hand over his short hair, he exhaled. The tension seemed to slowly leave his shoulders but his gaze stayed on something in the distance. "You have shopping to do. I can drop you at the market while I check the hardware store. How's that?"

"Look, can I just say again that I'm sorry?"

"No need."

This time she touched him, and he finally looked at her…at least at the hand she'd laid on his arm. "I would've been upset, too," she said, "if our roles were reversed. I wasn't thinking. Forgive me."

His short derisive laugh made her breath catch. "You don't need *my* forgiveness." He raised his gaze to her face, his eyes warming, and she felt her mouth relax into a smile. But he lingered too long on her lips, and instinctively she moistened them with her tongue.

"We should get going. I'll tell Gertrude…" Melanie pulled back her hand, but he caught it, closing his fingers around her wrist.

His hold was gentle, his eyes unwavering. "Do you live on this street?"

Her gaze automatically went to the row of small houses with their neatly trimmed lawns and cheery little flower beds. She suspected someone had to be looking out their window, curious about the stranger standing on Mrs. Wagner's porch and holding Pastor Ray's daughter captive. "The next one over."

Lucas loosened his grip but leaned closer. "Then I won't kiss you." A slight smile curved his mouth. "For now."

The September air was far too warm for the shiver that raced down her spine. Every instinct told her to pull free, step away from him. Surely that was what he expected her to do. She surprised them both by holding his gaze even when he released her and moved away first. "Why did you do that?"

"Do what?"

"It felt as though you were testing me."

He frowned. "How?"

Immediately she regretted her words. It was her. She'd overreacted to the saint reference. He wasn't seeing how far he could push her. Not like Rusty Smith had done after the eleventh-grade dance in order to win a bet. She'd actually thought Rusty liked her. That night in the school parking lot still ranked number one as the most humiliating experience of her life.

"Wow, I'm on a roll today." She briefly closed her eyes, then reluctantly looked at him. "Any chance we can just erase the last half hour?"

Lucas, bless him, gave her a slow easy smile. "I've never been one for dwelling on the past."

"Good. Excellent." She smiled back, earnestly looking forward to dinner at the Sundance with him. She didn't have to worry about the McAllisters. They weren't ones to judge. And after dinner? Thinking of the possibilities, she held back a sigh. "I'm going to grab Gertrude's shopping list and tell her what we're doing," she said, backing toward the door.

He didn't say a word, just nodded, his gaze running down her body. Not in a creepy or deliberate way. The appreciation in his eyes made her insides quiver. No man had ever looked at her like that before. Certainly no man as sexy and good-looking as Lucas.

It was a wonder she didn't trip hurrying back into the house.

Hearing Mrs. Wagner's voice, Melanie realized the woman was on the phone, probably talking to one of the Lemon sisters. Although she didn't mean to eavesdrop, she couldn't help hearing Lucas's name and her own. And then Mrs. Wagner's creaky laugh just before she lowered her voice.

Uh-oh. That wasn't good.

All Melanie had to do was noisily clear her throat or walk over the loose squeaky floorboard near the kitchen entrance. Instead she just stood in the doorway.

"Heavens, but you should see them together. They're just as cute as could be. Call her and invite them over. You'll see." Mrs. Wagner caught sight of her and straightened. "I have to go, Miriam. Talk to you later." She hung up the ancient wall phone behind her and turned to Melanie. "So you're still here. Figured you deserted me."

"You know I wouldn't do that. Where's your grocery list?"

Mrs. Wagner felt around in the pocket of her faded blue housedress and pulled out a slip of paper. The weekly items rarely varied, but she adjusted the bifocals that still gave her trouble after she'd worn them for thirty years and rechecked the list.

"While I shop, Lucas is going to the hardware store for a pipe so he can fix your sink," Melanie said, wondering if she should ignore what she'd guessed was going on or nip it in the bud. "Mrs. Wagner, I'm asking you very nicely—please don't play matchmaker."

She lifted her head, a puzzled frown on her craggy face. "What's that?"

"Lucas is a very nice man, but he's here on business. That's all." Melanie couldn't decide if the confusion on the woman's face was genuine or not. "No matchmaking, okay? I mean it."

"Oh, for pity's sake." She waved a hand. "The thought never entered my mind. Even I can see Lucas is too much man for you."

The pronouncement hit Melanie harder than a round of buckshot. She drew in a slow calming breath, feeling as helpless as a bird whose wings had been clipped. Luckily, she didn't have to put up a front. Gertrude had already gone back to reviewing her list. After all, the notion of Lucas and Melanie together was so absurd it didn't warrant another second of her time.

THE SUNDANCE WAS bustling with activity. Tendrils of smoke from the barbecue barrels drifted toward the cloudless blue sky, and even with the truck windows up, Lucas could smell charred mesquite and grilled steaks. Although it was possible his imagination was responding to his empty belly. The burger he'd grabbed at the diner after taking Melanie to Safe Haven to get her car hadn't been enough. Not after working all day.

He parked in the middle of a dozen or so rentals, cut the engine and turned to Melanie. Her attention was glued to a trio of women wearing skimpy sundresses and sipping drinks on the porch.

"You look really nice," he said and waited for her to face him. She'd been acting strange ever since they'd left Gertrude's, the first on a long list of stops they'd made throughout the afternoon. He'd expected her to bail on him tonight. That was why he'd insisted on bringing her with him.

She glanced down at her khaki shorts and stretchy blue tank top beneath an open white shirt. "Everyone's wearing dresses."

"That's because they're city folk and don't know any better."

Melanie looked at him and smiled. It faded as her gaze returned to the women. "Do you know most of them?"

"Me?" He picked up his Stetson. "Hell no. I got out of here as fast as I could this morning."

That made her laugh. "Better watch your step. Since they opened for guests, all three McAllister brothers have fallen hard and fast. Even Cole, the oldest. Shocked everyone for miles."

"Jesse and Shea? She was a guest?"

Melanie nodded. "Those boys broke the heart of every single woman in the county."

"Huh. Yours included?"

Surprise flickered in her eyes. "In high school I kind of had a thing for Trace. But so did every girl I knew." She shrugged, glancing toward the house. "It was nothing. Just an adolescent crush." She turned back to look at him. "If he's here, don't you dare tell him."

Lucas grinned, but it bothered him that she might still be interested in the guy. "He hook up with a guest, too?"

"No, he's with Matt's sister. Nikki's from Houston and Trace only met her this past February."

"And what about you, Melanie? How many hearts have *you* broken?"

She laughed. "Please."

The unmistakable sound of grinding gears grated on his ears and had him checking the rearview mirror. A woman driving a white compact pulled up behind them, then attempted to squeeze her car between his pickup and a silver sedan.

Melanie swiveled around, then just as quickly turned back to face him. "I can't look," she said, cringing. "Your poor truck. I don't think she's going to make it."

"This Ford and that tin can? Worry about her."

"Um, *I* managed to inflict some damage."

"Not much. And you tried with a whole bus."

"Hey, I wasn't *trying*...." Melanie bit her lip and peeked at him from under her thick dark lashes. "Is it safe to look? Did she make it?"

"Not yet." He had no idea what was happening with the compact. He was too interested in that lush lower lip of hers.

"Come here," he said, reaching across the console for her. "I'll protect you."

With a nervous laugh, she met his eyes, then slowly reared back.

"Yeah. Sorry." He plucked the grimy T-shirt away from his body. Since he'd waited in town to bring her back with him, he hadn't cleaned up yet. He needed a shower bad. But not bad enough that he'd been willing to give her the opportunity to stand him up.

"You're fine. I just didn't want—"

Their new neighbor slammed her door.

Melanie turned and watched the blonde wiggle out between cars, then start toward the house, stopping briefly to tug at her short denim skirt and fluff her hair.

Already Lucas was regretting the whole dinner thing. He'd had to push her to agree. Stupid of him not to have suggested they go someplace away from Blackfoot Falls. "You were saying...?"

Turning back to him, she took a deep breath and straightened her shoulders. "I think it's too warm for this shirt."

He watched her indecisively fidget with the unfastened buttons. "Probably," he agreed, trying not to sound too hopeful.

"If it gets chilly, I can always come get it." She let the shirt slip down her back but her arm got caught in it.

"Need help?"

"Would you?"

He reached over as she leaned forward, and he guided her elbow clear of the sleeve. It was easy after that. The shirt slid right off.

The blue top wasn't a tank. It had straps and dipped low in the back, showing off lots of creamy skin. She didn't have freckles, only a tiny mole by her left shoulder blade. The urge to touch her was so powerful that he jerked back as quickly as if he'd been burned.

"Thanks." She took the shirt and folded it in half. "Wait," she said when he started to open his door.

She calmly set the shirt aside, placed his Stetson on top, then got up on her knees so she could reach across the console and press her mouth to his.

8

MELANIE WISHED SHE could've been more graceful or at least not been trembling. But his lips were warm and gentle, reassuring her that she hadn't just made a fool of herself. She felt his hand close around her upper arm. His other one cupped the back of her neck, and he slanted his head, coaxing her lips apart.

Feeling the slightly rough texture of his tongue sent a shiver of pure longing down her spine. She leaned into him, or maybe he'd tugged her closer—she wasn't sure. Her heart pounded and her fingers itched to work their way under his shirt and touch his chest. But this wasn't the time or place.

There was only so much risk she was willing to take to shut out Gertrude's hurtful words. Melanie wasn't a child or completely inexperienced. And she sure wasn't a saint. She was, however, a normal red-blooded woman who was starting to melt under Lucas's practiced mouth.

He moved his hand down her back, his strong fingers a soothing hypnotic caress. His kiss grew more urgent, more demanding, more thrilling…until she realized he was trying to pull her onto his lap.

Heaven help her but she almost let him. Reluctantly, she

drew back, her breath catching at the hungry look on his face. "No," she whispered, miserable because she was the one who'd started this. "I'm sorry, but not here."

It took a few moments for his breathing to even out, a few more for him to let go of her arm. "You're right." His mouth curved in a faint smile and he brushed the hair back from her face. "Not out here."

She wondered if she'd shocked him. She'd only mildly surprised herself. Gertrude's words had simmered inside Melanie the whole afternoon. Admittedly, she wasn't exactly daring when it came to men, but she had more than her own reputation to worry about.

"We should go inside." She sat back, put her sandaled feet on the floorboard and smoothed her hair.

When he didn't say anything, she looked over at him. He didn't look happy, and she could feel his tension as intensely as if it were trying to drag her over the console.

He let out a strained laugh. "I'm gonna need another minute," he said and shifted against the seat.

She glanced at his fly. "Oh. Right," she murmured, turning away to hide her pleased smile. The Stetson had slid to the floor along with her shirt. She picked up his hat and tossed it on his lap. "Here you go."

Lucas chuckled and groaned at the same time. He tried to grab her but she plastered herself against her door until she could get it open and slide out. "Okay, I'll remember this," he muttered, setting the Stetson on his head.

Melanie laughed. She felt fifteen again. No, not fifteen. High school hadn't been much fun. Thirteen had been good. She'd still had friends back in the eighth grade. Boys had no longer had cooties, and she'd gone to her first coed dance. Never mind that it was with Laura and Rae Ann. They'd had a blast. It was the following year that Melanie had been dubbed *male repellant.*

He climbed out of the truck, pausing a moment before

he walked around the bed toward her. His lazy smile and loose gait didn't fool her. If she gave him an opening, he would retaliate. She backed up, bumping into the white compact.

"What are you going to do while I take a shower?" he asked, adjusting the Stetson and pulling the rim low enough to shadow his eyes.

"See if Rachel needs help."

"You've done enough good deeds today. How about you come join me instead?"

Melanie moved quickly to avoid being trapped against the car. "In the shower?"

"You can scrub my back."

"Thought I met my good-deed quota."

Lucas laughed. "What if I promise to make it worth your while?"

"You'll have to be more specific." She kept her tone light, casual, even as her racing pulse pumped her full of adrenaline.

"Well, now..." He used his forefinger to push up his Stetson. His eyes glittered with challenge. "Tell me what it would take and I'd be happy to oblige."

This wasn't at all like her, to be brazenly flirting. "Hmm, I suppose I should make it up to you for denting your fender."

"Better not be getting my hopes up for nothing."

The sound of excited chatter carried from the porch. Melanie turned and saw that a dozen or more women had come outside, along with Hilda, who had just set down a tray of tortilla chips and bowls of what had to be her prized salsa. Rachel poured frothy green margaritas into waiting glasses.

"I doubt you'll have a problem finding someone to scrub your back," Melanie said, picking up the pace, Lucas at her side. She nodded at the porch just as he caught the eye of a tall willowy brunette, who turned her smile on him. "You'll have them lining up."

Ignoring the woman, he leaned close to Melanie so that their shoulders touched. "You chickening out on me?" he whispered, his voice softly mocking.

She didn't dare look at him. "You knew I was joking."

"I wasn't."

Swallowing, she lifted a hand when Rachel glanced their way.

"Second floor, fourth door on the right," Lucas murmured when they reached the first step. "If you change your mind."

MELANIE HELPED RACHEL carry trays of food out to the picnic tables they used when the temperature was pleasant and the pests were minimal. Cole's girlfriend, Jamie, had already scouted out the grassy area butting up to a grove of rogue aspens, making sure the tables and benches were wiped off and free of unwelcome critters.

"This place looks like a mini park. Has it always been here?" Melanie asked, then laughed at Rachel's deadpan expression. "I don't mean the aspens."

"When was the last time you were out here?" Rachel set the bowl of potato salad next to the basket of corn bread.

"To the Sundance?" She thought for a moment. "Last year at your welcome-home party."

"Ah, before we opened for guests." Rachel nodded. "I promised my brothers I'd try to keep the women as separate as possible, so I spruced up this area for alfresco dining." She grinned. "That's how I describe it on the website."

Jamie had brought a bag of plates, silverware and napkins and stacked them at the end of the buffet table. "Problem is, the ladies only want to hang out where the guys are. I told Rachel we should make life-size cutouts of her brothers and post them at each table."

Melanie laughed.

Rachel glanced over her shoulder, then glared at Jamie. "Would you shut up?"

"They're too far away. No one heard." Jamie snorted. "Like you don't say stuff like that all the time."

"And by the way, quit butting into my welcome speech and telling them Cole is off-limits."

"I saw you making a 'taken' sign to put around Matt's neck when he comes over." Jamie filched a piece of corn bread and popped it into her mouth. Her appreciative moan stretched the limits of decency. "Damn, that's good."

"Wow, pretty convincing," Rachel said, looking impressed. "You must have to fake it a lot. Do I need to have a talk with my brother?"

Jamie grinned. "I'd like to hear that conversation."

Melanie had known Rachel her whole life and she didn't have that sort of easy camaraderie with her. Even while she enjoyed listening to the two of them, she felt envious and quite sad. Rachel hadn't been one of the girls who'd shunned her in school, but they'd never really been friends, either. At least Rachel never acted as if she had to watch her language or what she said around Melanie, so that was something.

And Jamie—she was someone Melanie would love to know better. But she'd moved to Blackfoot Falls only in January, and being a travel blogger, she was gone a lot. Luckily, Melanie got along well with Shea, though they really didn't socialize. Shea was an introvert with an IQ so high it would give most people nosebleeds. She was the first to admit she was socially awkward. That she'd ended up with Jesse still stunned Melanie and probably a lot of other people, including Shea. But the match also gave Melanie hope. Maybe there was a man out there for her, too.

Second floor, fourth door on the right.

Good grief—her head was about to explode. How many times were Lucas's words going to blindside her? Or worse, get her so worked up.

Both women were staring at her, so obviously she'd let something slip. A cuss word, maybe. A frustrated sigh? It didn't matter. She didn't see shock in their faces, mostly amusement. Had either one of them been in her place, they would've jumped all over Lucas's offer.

"Um, earworm," she murmured. "The stupid song's driving me crazy. Should I go get more food from Hilda?"

Grinning, Jamie looked past her. "I think your man's got that covered."

"My what?" Melanie turned to find Lucas coming from the house surrounded by four women, all of them balancing bowls and platters.

He barely smiled, just enough to be polite. Clearly he wasn't thrilled with the attention. And that made her a lot happier than it should have.

"I hadn't planned on putting you ladies to work," Rachel said when the group got closer. "Well, not your first night here, anyway." Reaching to take the platter of grilled meat from Lucas, she tried to hide a grin. "Good job."

"My pleasure," he said in a tone that indicated it was anything but. "You got this?"

"Got it," Rachel said, and he let go of the platter. Then she moved close enough to him to privately murmur, "Don't say I didn't warn you," before she turned her smile on the guests.

If Rachel weren't engaged to Matt, Melanie would have been jealous. She hated the thought. Hated that she was still a little jealous anyway. Rachel had purposely spoken loud enough to include her in the joke, but that wasn't the point. Melanie wasn't the jealous type. Yet she wanted

Lucas all to herself. She wanted to be able to exchange a private look with him, share a joke no one else understood.

"May I borrow you for a moment?"

She blinked at the warm hand on her arm and then met his gaze. She could smell the freshness of his shower on his skin, saw that he'd shaved. Without thinking, she lifted her hand and touched his smooth jaw.

The outside corners of his eyes crinkled with his smile. Before she could snatch her hand back, he caught and held it to his face, turning his head so his lips dragged across her palm. Then he slowly brought his gaze back to hers. They were standing in the middle of a bunch of strange women. She didn't know who'd just sighed or which one said, "Hubba-hubba."

Someone else said, "Dammit, I thought he was here alone."

"Well?" he said, paying no attention to anyone but her. His eyes remained on her face and his hand stayed pressed to hers as she lowered it.

Not for the life of her could she recall what he'd asked.

"If she's not interested, you can borrow me," the blonde said, getting a laugh from the others.

Melanie glanced around, searching out Rachel.

"Go," she said, before Melanie could ask if she needed help.

Lucas took her hand and led her into the aspens. She felt the stares burning into her back, and it was horrible to acknowledge the deep sense of satisfaction at knowing some of those women were jealous of *her*. Truly horrible. Her father would be appalled. Melanie was appalled. Or at least, she was trying to be.

"Where are we going?" she asked, too breathless for such a short walk.

"I only wanted to pull you aside, but this is better."

"Better for what?"

He took them another few feet, then framed her face with his hands. For a long heart-stopping moment he did nothing but look into her eyes. "I was hoping you'd surprise me."

"The shower? I couldn't."

His gaze lowered to her mouth. "I know," he said, moving his hands to her shoulders. "I shouldn't be teasing you."

"Of course you should."

A lazy smile started slowly, curving his mouth and making her pulse race. "I *should* be kissing you instead."

And that was exactly what he did. She tipped her head back, softening her lips as he moved over them. He didn't try to coax her mouth open but seemed content learning the taste and shape of her lips as if this were their first kiss. She was the one who touched her tongue to his and got him worked up. He slid his hands down her back, stopping just at the curve of her backside. Slanting his head to deepen the kiss, he pulled her against his aroused body.

She shoved her hands up his chest, lightly digging into hard muscle with her short nails, and moved her hips against him. He shuddered. Then stopped kissing her. Just stopped. He pulled his arms from around her and caught her wrists, holding her hands still, trapping them so she couldn't touch him.

Melanie reluctantly looked up at him.

His nostrils flared and his eyes were hooded.

Muted laughter came from the picnic area. Probably nothing to do with them. No one could see this deep into the trees. But if anyone had come looking, she doubted she would've heard anything.

Lucas stroked the wildly beating pulse at her wrist. "I shouldn't have pulled you away," he said, his breathing ragged. "But I've been thinking about kissing you all day."

When she finally found her voice, it spilled out a husky whisper. "Me too."

"Can we leave?" He released her wrists and stroked his thumb down her cheek. "Would Rachel mind?"

Longing swelled inside her. She briefly closed her eyes and leaned into his touch. "I can't. It would bother me," she admitted, pulling back and lowering her arms to her sides. "I'm sorry."

"Yeah." His gaze caught on her lips and lingered. "I wouldn't feel right, either." He smiled. "Now, eating dessert someplace else is another story."

That startled a laugh out of her. "Did you just want to kiss me, or was there something else?"

He tucked a lock of hair behind her ear. "I already got my answer," he said, taking her by the shoulders and turning her toward the path.

"What?" Curious, she squirmed away from his touch and looked at him. "Come on. Tell me."

"I want to strip you naked and make love to you for hours."

Melanie laughed, wishing the heat surging up her neck would go away. "Come on…. Really."

He took her hand and pressed it to his fly. "Really," he whispered, and this time she believed him.

"SO, LUCAS, HOW BIG is your ranch?" Joanna was a court reporter from Los Angeles or San Diego…. Melanie couldn't remember which. All she knew for sure was that the nosy new arrival had planted herself directly across the table from them and seemed to have a million and one questions.

So far she'd found out that Lucas was thirty-two, from Wyoming, had spent a lot of time in Denver recently, owned a ranch, had attended college for two years before he decided it wasn't for him, then later finished his degree online. Also that his only sister lived in Atlanta with her husband and new baby, and his mother and stepfather retired to Florida five years ago. He saw all of them a couple of times a year.

On the one hand, Melanie felt terrible for him. He'd handled the barrage of questions with grace and sometimes humor, but it couldn't be pleasant. She wasn't the one in the hot seat and she was feeling uncomfortable.

On the other hand, Melanie had learned more about him in the past ten minutes than she had in the thirty-some hours since she'd met him.

"Lucas, how big is your ranch?" Joanna repeated. "As big as the Sundance?"

He shook his head and kept chewing.

"Then how big is it?"

His patience was slipping. Melanie could see it now. First the nonverbal answers and the stiffening of his shoulders, then the tiny tic in his jaw.

"The Sundance is the second-largest ranch in the county," Melanie said, hoping to redirect the conversation. "About three thousand acres, I think. The McAllisters have been here for close to a hundred and fifty years."

"Yeah, that's all on the website," Joanna said without taking her gaze off Lucas. "So how many acres do you have?"

For a moment he didn't say a word. "Four hundred."

"Do you have horses, cows, the whole bit?"

He put his fork down. "You mentioned you're a court reporter," he said, and she nodded, appearing pleased he was taking an interest in her. "You should've been a lawyer. You ask enough questions."

Joanna grinned. "I've heard that before."

The other women hid nervous smiles.

Rachel was sitting at another table but must've been listening. She got up, brought over a pitcher of iced tea and asked Joanna about the weather in San Diego and then something about shopping across the Mexican border, which gave Lucas a reprieve. A very short one.

Joanna answered quickly, then turned back to him. "So, I'm curious, did you grow up on a ranch? I mean, how else do you learn how to run one, right?"

He'd picked up his fork again and was finishing his corn.

"God, Joanna, let the poor guy eat." Her friend Vanessa had barely spoken, not that she'd had a chance.

"I'm just curious." Joanna gave her a chilly glare. "How will I learn anything if I don't ask questions?"

Melanie put her arm around Lucas's shoulder and gently rubbed the tense muscles. If she'd surprised him, he didn't let it show. He turned to her with a lazy smile as if it was the most natural thing in the world for her to be touching him.

She wasn't quite as relaxed. There was nothing normal about her cozying up to a man in public. But if she was going to do it anywhere in Blackfoot Falls, this was the easiest place for her to be herself.

Odd thought, though she had no time to analyze it.

"Oh. I didn't—" Joanna cut herself off. How refreshing. "You two are together?" she asked, swinging her disappointed expression from Melanie to Lucas.

Laughter erupted at Joanna's clueless reaction, though to be fair, she'd come after their little disappearing act into the woods.

Lucas ignored her. He ignored everyone. Anyone watching would think he had eyes only for Melanie. Of course, she knew the idea was absurd but it was still thrilling.

"So, Melanie, I assumed you were from Blackfoot Falls," Joanna said. "Where did you guys meet?"

Still looking at Lucas, Melanie bit her lip and then just laughed. She couldn't help herself.

Lucas shook his head, sharing in her amusement. Then he turned to the woman. "Joanna," he said. "Eat."

Her jaw slackened. "Well, excuse me. I'm only trying to make conversation." She picked up her half-full glass. "More tea, please," she said to Rachel, who'd already moved on to another table.

She returned with the pitcher and poured with a smile. "Mel, are you finished? Would you mind giving me a hand?"

Rachel walked over to the buffet table and started cutting a chocolate sheet cake into squares. "Sorry about this," she murmured under her breath as soon as Melanie joined her. "I'm gonna kill Trace and Jesse. They were supposed to have dinner with us." She sighed. "Probably better they didn't." She sneaked a peek at Joanna. "That girl may have the honor of being the first guest I throw out on her ass."

"You wouldn't do that." Melanie looked in the bag Jamie had left and found small paper plates. Her gaze drifted over to Lucas. His back was to her but he turned right at that moment and winked. For a second, she completely forgot what she was doing. Ah, the paper plates. "Are you using these for the cake?"

Rachel nodded. "Poor Lucas. If you guys want to shove off, I don't blame you."

"Is Jamie coming back out to help you clean up?"

"I'll be fine. Go on. Maybe you two can have dinner with Matt and me before Lucas leaves town. We'll eat at the Lone Wolf. In peace."

"You know there's nothing going on between us, right?"

"Well, there should be." Rachel was quick with the spatula, filling the plates as fast as Melanie set them out. "Lucas is obviously into you. And I have never seen you put your arm around a man under eighty."

Melanie groaned. "I was being polite and defending him."

"Uh-huh." Rachel grinned. "Get out of here. Go defend him someplace in private."

Melanie felt her cheeks heat. Rachel was blushing, too. But she always did, even when she wasn't embarrassed. "I'll help you pass out the cake first."

"Go. Now." Rachel took a plate out of her hand. "That being said, I'm so glad you came. I wish I had a mute button for some of the guests, but hey…." She shrugged. "Now scoot."

Melanie nodded and turned to Lucas. He was already headed toward her, his determined smile making her breath catch.

9

LUCAS STOPPED THE TRUCK at the end of the driveway. No one was coming down the gravel road. He was free to make the turn that would take them to Blackfoot Falls. But he wasn't ready to say good-night to Melanie, and he had the feeling that once they entered the town limits, everything would change between them. She'd go back to being shy and nervous, constantly on guard.

It reminded him of how he'd felt in prison that first year. Always watching, waiting, wondering who might be lying low for him. Except Melanie was the town do-gooder. She seemed to like feeling needed. Him, he'd been full of rage and confusion and looking for release. Spending his time beefing up and seeking answers with his fists. What a hell of a year.

She turned expectantly to him. "What are you waiting for?"

"The stars."

"What?" Laughing, she looked up at the sky through the windshield. "I see some, but it's not dark enough yet. There'll be a whole slew of them in another hour."

"You don't realize how much you take them for granted

until you can't see them," he said, searching between the scudding clouds.

"Did you have a different iced tea than the rest of us?" she said, sitting back with a laugh.

He looked over at her. She sure was pretty with her dark hair and pink cheeks. "I wanted to apologize to Rachel before we left, but I figured that might make things worse. I'll do it later."

"What on earth do you have to apologize for?"

"I should've been more patient with Joanna."

"Are you kidding? She was horrible and rude and made everyone uncomfortable. Rachel was so irritated, I wouldn't be surprised if she said something to her."

Leaning back, he stretched out his arm and idly twirled a lock of her hair around his finger. "Were *you* uncomfortable?"

"Me? I hated that you were cornered by all those questions."

"I didn't have to answer."

She hesitated. "Were you telling the truth? I mean, did you make things up just to—? Never mind." She glanced over her shoulder. "Seriously, why are we just sitting here?"

"I'm trying to figure out which way to go."

"There's only one highway." Melanie paused to moisten her lips with a slow swipe of her tongue. She'd probably hate to know what that just did to him. "It takes you in and out of town."

"Is that where we want to go?"

"I don't know but we better decide. I think those are headlights coming from the Sundance."

He checked the side mirror, put the truck in gear and drove. Maybe she was fine with their night ending in the twenty minutes it would take him to drop her off. He didn't believe that, not after the kiss earlier. But with Melanie being the town good girl and all… And they'd only just met… Was it yesterday?

Damn, it didn't seem possible. He did the math. Yep, he'd arrived yesterday. Still didn't seem possible.

"How about the Watering Hole?" he asked, figuring she'd prefer a more public place.

"What about it?"

"Want to have a drink? Wait for those stars to show up?" He waited for her response and got nothing but silence. Finally, he turned to look at her, only to find her frowning and worrying her lip. "Does the bar get rowdy on Saturdays? We don't have to go there."

"I've never been." She sounded surprised, which didn't make sense. "I mean, I've been inside but only twice, for Safe Haven board meetings. Sadie's the owner. She lets us meet there before the bar opens."

Lucas wasn't sure what to think. Some people never went to bars, he supposed. For a solid year he'd been so busy fixing up his ramshackle ranch he hadn't stepped foot in a bar or even a restaurant. He hadn't had the time or money. But Blackfoot Falls was a small town with limited entertainment, and she'd lived here all her life.

"You have something against the Watering Hole?" he asked. "Or bars in general?"

"Neither." She shrugged. "No one's ever asked me to go and I certainly wouldn't go in by myself. Especially now with all the Sundance guests— Oh, we'd probably run into Joanna."

"Ah, shit." Lucas winced. "Sorry."

Melanie laughed. "I was thinking the same thing."

"Yep, we're skipping anyplace in town." They were about five minutes away, and he was hoping she'd invite him to her house.

"There's really nothing from here to Kalispell. And it's too late to go that far."

He glanced at the dash clock. Only eight-thirty. "What, no sleeping in on Sundays?"

She sighed. "Sleep in? What's that?"

"Safe Haven? I can help with feeding the animals."

"Tomorrow's covered. I'll be busy with church stuff," she said, her voice low and tentative. "Driving Gertrude and Pauline to morning service, for one thing."

Hell, Melanie really was a saint. Shopping, cooking, chauffeuring, and for a bunch of opinionated old ladies. He'd met four of them. "I'd bet good money that Pauline rides shotgun and tells you when to brake, when to turn and how to park."

She laughed. "Every Sunday. Care to join us?"

"Gee, I'd like to help you out but…"

"Coward."

"A smart man knows when to stand down. I'm not tangling with those two."

"They're really very sweet. Usually." Sighing, she relaxed against the leather headrest. "And time-consuming."

"Hey. I was teasing." He caught her hand. "You know I'll help if you need me."

Melanie straightened. "I wasn't complaining. They're part of my routine.… I don't mind." Slowly she turned her hand over so their palms met. "You're welcome to go to service with us if you want." She paused, waiting for his response, stiffening at his silence. "I don't know if you even attend—" She cleared her throat. "We have three denominations in the area, if you need directions."

"I won't." He'd lost his faith the day the judge passed down his sentence. Man, he'd been naive. Hard to admit now. He'd done the right thing, never dreaming he would get locked up for it.

They'd already entered town. He released her hand to grab the wheel, kind of surprised she hadn't pulled away first. He should've figured her for a churchgoer. Didn't matter to him. But he had a feeling his lack of interest mattered to Melanie.

He knew her street was coming up, but they hadn't decided on what to do next. It had to be her call. He hoped the evening would end with more than a few kisses.

"It's on the left," she said softly, and that settled it. She obviously wanted to go home, and he doubted she'd be leaving the light on for him.

Right before he made the turn, he saw a carload of Sundance guests coming up behind them. Hell, he couldn't even go to the bar and get drunk in peace.

He pulled up in front of the small yellow house with its white picket fence and neatly trimmed yard. A wooden swing hung from the porch beams and a big pot of pink mums sat on the first step. Her home looked like a happy and safe place. Very Melanie.

And not like anything in his life. Or his future. Prison had taken care of that.

It was just as well they ended the night here. He still wanted Safe Haven's cooperation in fostering mustangs, maybe letting PRN take some of the abandoned mares they were housing. Melanie believed in the program and thought Shea would be on board, too. He'd stick around since he had nowhere else to be for another week. He saw no reason why they couldn't continue to work together. Maybe he'd even donate some time and muscle to building the new corral Levi had mentioned. But socializing? Her time and energy were limited. She wouldn't want to waste them on the likes of him.

"Well, thank you." She'd turned to him while patting the door behind her, searching for the handle. "I wish we could've seen more stars."

Lucas smiled, sadness mounting inside him like a persistent toothache. It hadn't even occurred to her that they could spend the next few hours doing just that. When he couldn't stand it another second, he leaned over to stop her fumbling.

She gasped, jerking back, then relaxed when she saw he'd meant only to lift the handle for her. The tip of her tongue slipped out to moisten her lips as it had earlier, and he had to look away.

"I'll wait until you get inside," he murmured, listening to the engine idle.

"It's Blackfoot Falls, for heaven's sake. You don't have to."

"I know."

"Lucas?" Her voice shook, breaching his resolve to not look at her. "Did you want to come in?"

Even with her face in shadow he could see her uncertainty. "Do you want me to?"

As if on cue, her neighbor's porch light came on. Melanie jerked a look at it. Across the street the front door of a brick house opened. An older man stepped outside, peering intently at them. He couldn't see past the tinted windows. Wouldn't shock Lucas if the guy walked over and pressed his nose to the glass.

"They don't recognize your truck," she said, her shoulders sagging. "Well, guess you don't have to wait for me to get inside." She tried to sound cheery. Considering the remark meant her invitation was no longer on the table.

It was okay. He got it. A small town like this and Melanie being a young single schoolteacher… What did he expect? His fault for getting his hopes up again. The town good girl wouldn't be caught dead with a guy like him.

"Go," he said. "Before they call the sheriff."

"Oh, Lord, they probably will." She pushed the door open, then glanced back at him. "I should kiss you. Give them all a show."

Lucas just smiled. They both knew she wouldn't dare.

She grabbed the white shirt she'd discarded earlier,

climbed out and waved to the nosy man across the street. Apparently that wasn't enough for him. He stood on his porch with his arms crossed over his paunch. Probably would stay right there until Lucas left. Something he had no intention of doing until Melanie was safely inside the house.

He watched her mount the front steps, briefly stooping to pluck a withered leaf from the pink mums. She looked good in the long khaki shorts and blue top. Nice shapely legs, toned arms, smooth creamy skin… He sure liked the way she felt in his arms, all feminine and curvy, and damn, but her hair was soft. She'd be tentative in bed, he guessed, but only at first. With the right man, the right touch…

Jesus, what the hell was wrong with him? By no stretch was he the right man. Not for someone like her. He should be buying her neighbor a beer for interrupting them. How many times did Lucas have to remind himself he wanted only uncomplicated sex? He had a thick skull—he'd admit it—but he wasn't usually this stupid. That woman defined *complicated.* A churchgoing do-gooder. Yeah, just what he needed. The calculating do-gooders he knew in Denver—those were the kind of women for him. From now on his dealings with Melanie had to be strictly business related.

Sweat gathered at the back of his neck and he threw the truck out of Park. Why was she just standing at the door? He knew it wasn't locked.

She glanced back at him, nibbling that lush lower lip of hers, then turned and hurried toward the truck.

If he had a lick of sense he'd just take off. Pretend he hadn't seen her. With the tinted windows, she wouldn't know otherwise. She pulled the door open.

"What?"

At his harsh tone she jumped. Too bad it didn't scare her into the house. She blinked, then smiled as if she knew his bark didn't mean he'd bite. Thinking she knew him was going to get her in trouble.

"Come to dinner tomorrow," she said, her lips lifting in an excited smile.

"Here?"

"Yes, here. I'll put leashes on the neighbors."

He slid a look at the house next to hers. The porch light was still on. "You sure?"

"I am. Is six okay? Six-thirty?"

"Tell me when—I'll be here."

"Five-thirty," she said and laughed. Her cheeks were flushed, her eyes bright.

Dammit, he wanted to kiss her. "Five-thirty," he agreed and started to sweat in earnest.

"THANK YOU, BUT I have plans," she said for the fifth time. It seemed half the congregation wanted her over for supper. She really, really hoped it was a coincidence and had nothing to do with Lucas. Sometimes she hated living in a small town.

Shirley clutched the brim of her big white hat, saving it from the stiff breeze. With her free hand she took Melanie's arm and drew her toward the shady side of the stone church where her father had just delivered his sermon on tolerance. "You're not working on a Sunday, are you?"

Oh, brother.

Yes, this was absolutely about Lucas. If Shirley wanted to chitchat, it was always with Melanie's mother, not Melanie. Unless Shirley was being nosy. Like right now.

"I'm sorry, Shirley, would you excuse me? I think Gertrude and Pauline are looking for their ride." She waved at the two women, who frowned at her for disturbing their weekly in-person gossip session with the Lemon sisters. "I'll see you next Sunday." She rushed off, leaving Shirley gaping after her. Oh, well—she'd get over it.

"Melanie. Wait."

She all but froze at the sound of David's deep husky voice behind her. It was the only thing about him she found appealing. At least in a sexual way. He was her boss, and he'd been supportive of her efforts to use Safe Haven as a teaching medium. She appreciated his willingness to try new things. Her former principal, whom David had replaced a year ago, had refused to entertain any sort of change.

Unfortunately, it was becoming more and more apparent that gratitude and respect weren't what David wanted from her.

Pasting on a smile, she turned to him. He seemed pale, or maybe that was his natural coloring and she hadn't paid that much attention. "You're here. I didn't see you during the service."

"I was in the back. Had a late start this morning." He always wore a suit to church even though no one else did. His shoes were polished and his hair combed straight back. The man took pride in his appearance—she'd give him that. He even drove all the way to Kalispell for his haircuts. "Fine sermon your father gave." David smiled. "As always."

"Yes, he does have a gift." She leaned toward him, too late realizing she'd opened herself up to be misunderstood. "Other pastors used to put me to sleep when I was a kid," she whispered and quickly drew back, but not before he felt sufficiently comfortable to touch her arm.

His smile was pleasant, his blue eyes unremarkable. They were nothing remotely like Lucas's color. She banished the errant thought. This wasn't a competition.

"I was wondering if you'd like to have lunch," he said, taking his hand from her arm. "Not alone." He cleared his throat, the neutral smile back in place. "The Andersons invited us over."

"Oh, how thoughtful of them, but I can't." She glanced over at Gertrude and Pauline. No doubt they wanted to linger, but she had to get out of here. "Please give the Andersons my regrets."

"Melanie." He caught her arm. "How about dinner? We could go to Kalispell. No one would have to know," he added in a low voice. "Not that I'm suggesting anything unprofessional. But I am your boss and I know how people talk."

She'd known this moment was coming. He'd asked her to coffee a few times, and she'd even gone once, though she'd kept the conversation about work. Same thing whenever they'd shared a table in the teachers' lounge for lunch. Asking her to dinner was different. So was his steady gaze, as if he was dissecting every facet of her reaction.

"I can't," she said simply. "I have plans."

He wasn't pleased. "Another time perhaps?"

"Sure." She could tell he didn't believe her. That was fine. Let him think what he wanted. He'd started coming to church only six months ago, after he'd tried and failed to start getting personal with her. And worse, he'd become chummy with her father. "I'll see you at school tomorrow, huh?"

She smiled and left to say a quick goodbye to her mother. Today she was too excited to stand around listening to everyone sing her father's praises. She wanted to get home and start dinner. Not that she was making an elaborate meal to impress Lucas. She was a decent cook, and her standard pot roast would be perfectly sufficient. What she wanted was to be out of the kitchen before he arrived. Shea was returning tomorrow, and tonight might be the last time Melanie would have Lucas to herself.

The thought was almost enough to depress her. She slowed her breathing, slowed her hurried steps. No good would come of her becoming too wrapped up with Lucas.

Yes, he'd shown interest in her. She had no doubt tonight could end up with him discovering she had a truly terrific mattress.

Heavens, she couldn't even *think* the word *sex.* Not right in front of the church. And her father. She stopped several feet from her mother. LaDonna Knowles was the perfect minister's wife. She always knew the proper thing to say, always dressed the part, lent an ear to anyone who needed her, and she always, without fail, put her husband and the church first.

Melanie wasn't at all like her, no matter what people seemed overly fond of repeating. It wasn't that she couldn't live up to her mother's selflessness. Melanie didn't want to be that person. She was deeply grateful to have been raised to be kind and generous. She just didn't want to completely give up her own life. Be scrutinized and judged by everyone who knew her. She doubted anyone, including her parents, had forgiven her for moving to town to be on her own.

She briefly squeezed her eyes shut. Was she being a complete fool? Was this some ridiculous rebellion that would end up biting her in the behind? She might not be the image of her mom, but it wasn't like her to be this twisted up over a man, a stranger even, who was totally out of her league. He'd be gone soon, and life would be tedious and predictable again. And possibly minus the cushion of her "good girl" reputation. And what about her Safe Haven project? If she made David angry, he could shut her down.

No, she was letting nerves get the better of her. Everyone knew she was involved with Safe Haven. It was reasonable for her to have Lucas over for dinner. She wouldn't be reckless about it. People would see his truck. They'd know he was at her house. She'd shoo him out before dark. What happened between five-thirty and eight-thirty would be only speculation on the part of her neighbors. She could live with that.

She spotted Gertrude laughing it up with the Lemon sisters, all of them wearing their Sunday best. Gertrude and Pauline would object to being rushed, but too bad. Melanie caught her mother's eye. She smiled and gave a small nod, as if she knew Melanie was anxious to leave.

"Okay, ladies, your driver doesn't have all day," she said as she approached the group, bracing herself for their protest.

The Lemon twins and Pauline either hadn't heard or were ignoring her. Not Gertrude, though. She looked Melanie up and down, then gave her a peculiar smile.

"Why? You got a hot date with that hunk of yours?" The question alone was surprising. But that Gertrude lowered her voice so only Melanie could hear was the shocker.

"And what if I do?"

"I'd say it's about damn time someone lit a fire under you." Gertrude hitched her shawl up over her shoulders and gripped her walker. "Come on, Pauline. Quit yakking. We've gotta hit the road."

10

LUCAS HAD SHAVED AGAIN. Two days in a row. His overworked razor was likely to go on strike. He parked the truck in the same place where he'd sat idling last night and walked to Melanie's front door.

She opened it before he knocked. "You're right on time."

"Hi." He waited for her to move. She stayed put. "Are you going to let me in?"

"Oh, yes, of course." She sighed and rolled her eyes as she backed up. Today her shorts were black and shorter than the khaki ones. Her feet were bare. He hid a smile at her bright pink toenails.

Her red button-down blouse was more conservative and tucked neatly into her waistband. He wondered if her bra was red, too, and lacy, then wondered if he was going to find out. Man, he had to stop that train. This was only dinner.

So far.

"I thought about bringing wine or flowers," he muttered, only now remembering his hat. He yanked it off. "But I figured you wouldn't want this looking like a date. To your neighbors."

Goddammit, he was nervous all of a sudden.

“Thank you.” Her smile lit the room. “That was thoughtful,” she said, motioning for him to follow her. “People around here are weird.”

“Not all of them.”

She was so quick to look over her shoulder that she caught him checking out her butt. He shifted his gaze, pretending interest in the hook rug covering the hardwood floor, then studied the floral couch and sturdy oak coffee table.

“Nice place,” he murmured and met her eyes.

She was trying not to laugh.

“What?”

The dam broke. She pressed her lips together but she was already laughing too hard, and not in a particularly ladylike fashion. “I’m nervous, okay? I laugh when I’m nervous. I can’t help it.”

“No need to be jumpy. It’s just dinner.” Now that he’d found a measure of cool after being jittery himself, he had some nerve. “Right?”

She stopped long enough for him to see the yearning in her brown eyes, the slight parting of her lips. His good intentions, the vow he’d made to keep the evening platonic… Everything vanished. He sent his Stetson sailing toward the couch and reached for her. She came willingly into his arms, drawing in a shuddering breath. The vibration echoed in his chest when she pressed against him.

Her nipples were tight and hard enough he could feel them through the layers of their clothing. She hugged his neck, pressing her body closer when he cupped her rounded bottom with both hands and took her with an openmouthed kiss. She was more than ready, her eager tongue warm and welcoming, her soft sexy whimper stoking a fire low in his belly.

He had to slow himself down. Slow them both down before they leaped into something she wasn’t ready for.

Another minute and he wouldn't be able to think clearly. Skimming his hands up her back, he tried to gentle the kiss. But she tasted too good, felt too good and smelled too good. He had to go cold turkey.

Gripping her upper arms, he set her away from him.

The sound of their harsh breathing seemed to echo off the walls and fill the house. She blinked, looking confused, disoriented, swiftly dissolving into humiliation. Averting her eyes, she jerked a shoulder, trying to free her arm.

"Hey." He caught her chin and brought her gaze back to his. "I'm sorry I pushed."

"I think it was the other way around. But thanks."

"We'll call it a draw," he said, and she gave him a small shy smile. Releasing her chin, he trailed his thumb along the line of her delicate jaw, then brushed the hair away from her flushed cheeks. He knew better. Knew damn well he should've moved out of reach. Trust him to keep his hand in the fire. "You smell good."

"I think that's the pot roast."

He smiled. "I believe I know the difference."

Her lips twitched and she started to say something, then apparently reconsidered. "I think the roast is done," she said, leading him into the airy kitchen. "What did you do today?"

Watching the slight sway of her hips and catching glimpses of her pink toenails weren't doing him any favors. His jeans were still too snug even after adjusting his fly. He forced himself to check out the kitchen. The light tan paint job looked new, and he could easily picture Melanie standing on a ladder, patiently applying the blue-and-white stenciled border a few inches from the white ceiling. She'd be wearing old denim cutoffs that rode low on her hips and showed a lot of shapely leg.

Okay, that hadn't gone as planned.

He saw her expectant frown and realized she'd asked

him a question. "I spent a few hours at Safe Haven." He glanced around again. "How long have you lived here?"

"Six months." She lifted the lid off a pot on the stove and used a long wooden spoon to stir the contents. "What were you doing out there?"

"Talking to Levi and Kathy." The hearty aroma of stewing meat reminded him he hadn't eaten since breakfast. "Is all this your handiwork?" he asked, gesturing to the walls.

"Yep. And most of the tiled floor.... I will never, ever, ever do that again. I ended up having to pay someone to fix my mistakes." She shrugged. "Next I'm tackling the countertop. I really hate this yellow Formica."

Lucas smiled. No one could call her a quitter. "Ever done a counter?"

"No." She sounded slightly defensive. Then her shoulders sagged. "Will I regret it?"

"I did when I renovated the fixer-upper I bought. But then, I'm not the most patient guy." He hadn't meant to bring up the ranch. It still hurt to talk about it, to remember how his dream had gone up in smoke as sure as if it'd been consumed by wildfire.

"Any tips?"

"Yeah. Hire a professional."

Melanie laughed. "On a teacher's salary? I don't think so."

"As you found out, you screw it up and you end up paying anyway."

"I did all right with the paint job and stenciling," she said with a defiant lift of her chin.

"Or you could benefit from my mistakes and let me help you." It was the wrong thing to say. He'd decided to stay for a week. Thinking of anything beyond that was plain foolish. He was an ex-con with a limited future. "That was dumb," he said with a shrug. "I don't know when you plan on ripping all this up." He fingered the Formica, studying the seams just so he didn't have to look at Melanie's stunned expression. "Who knows where I'll be?"

"I'll have to get permission from my landlord." She'd turned back to the stove and fiddled with the controls. "He wasn't happy about letting me remove the wallpaper even though it was older than dirt."

"So you're renting? I don't know why I assumed you owned the house."

"I suppose I should think about buying." Her tone lacked enthusiasm. "There are tax advantages."

"Not a good reason to sign your life over to a mortgage company. You should love the place."

She nodded thoughtfully, then looked at him. "Do you love your ranch? Was it worth pouring your heart and soul into it?"

The question shouldn't have surprised him but it still made him tense. It was her trusting brown eyes that got to him. Cocooned here in a community that loved her, did she even know how ugly life could turn in an instant? "I did once," he said and saw hurt flicker in her eyes. Hurt for him. "Maybe someday I will again."

He didn't believe that for a second. She seemed to, though—a little bit, anyway—and that was good enough. For both of them. He didn't need her feeling sorry for him. His actions had cost him his freedom and his future. Put to the test, he'd do it all over again. It was his own ass. He wouldn't drag anyone to hell with him.

She hadn't turned back to the stove and her troubled expression was starting to get under his skin. It was the way she was looking at him, as if she feared saying the wrong thing would make him explode.

It took a moment for him to realize he was clenching his jaw. He could feel the dark thoughts eclipsing his mood. It happened sometimes, no matter how hard he tried not to think of the past. The people he worked with in Denver understood, and they just stayed away from him until the brief bouts passed.

Not Melanie.

She smiled gently. "I hope so. I hope you find joy again," she said, then opened a drawer and took out a fork. She speared a piece of meat, and cupping her hand under it, she brought the sample to his lips. "Tell me what you think. I can still add more seasoning."

She waited for him to open his mouth. She hadn't run from his mood. From him. Instead she fed him pot roast.

MELANIE WASN'T SURE if his slow smile was specifically designed to make her knees weak or if it simply meant he liked the taste. "Well?"

"Perfect."

"I can add more salt or pepper. It won't hurt my feelings if you think it's too bland."

Shaking his head, he put his hands on her waist. His gaze locked on hers.

"Okay, then." She flipped the fork over her shoulder and hoped it landed in the sink. "Gertrude knew."

"Knew what?"

"That I was seeing you tonight."

His only reaction was a slight lift of his right brow. "What did she say?"

"Something like 'it's about damn time.'" Melanie slid her hands up his chest, feeling the deep rumble of his quiet laughter under her palms, and grabbed a fistful of his button-down shirt. "You know the best thing about pot roast?"

"Tell me."

Neither of them broke eye contact. "You don't have to eat it right away." She pulled him down and brushed a kiss across his lips. "It's still good an hour later."

"Or three."

"Or three," she agreed, her attempt to sound matter-of-fact coming out a hoarse whisper.

Lucas hadn't moved his hands, which rested loosely at her waist. His flaring nostrils were the only evidence he hadn't been carved from stone. "Are you sure about this?"

She didn't have to think about it, because she'd been doing that all day. Caught in his unwavering gaze, she lost her ability to speak. A nod didn't seem adequate, so she tugged him closer while she stretched up on her toes. Her kiss would have to convince him this was what she wanted.

Their lips met and he pulled her against him. He was already hard, and the thrill of that knowledge shimmered down her spine.

She rubbed her aching nipples against his chest, feeling a slight shudder pass through him. He used his tongue to part her lips, then slowly swept inside.

He was so very wrong about not being a patient man. He took his time, learning her mouth and letting her adjust to his tender exploration, almost in deference to her limited experience. Though he couldn't know about that, he certainly might've guessed. He understood small towns, knew she valued her reputation. Or perhaps he found her skills to be lacking.

The thought momentarily unsettled her. No, she wouldn't let anything ruin tonight. She wanted this; she wanted Lucas. And she had no doubt he wanted her.

His heart pounded as fiercely as hers, and his mouth was no longer so gentle. Pulling her blouse free of her shorts, he slipped his hands underneath and ran his rough palms up her back. Her skin tingled. She waited, clutching his shoulders, wondering if he would unhook her bra when his fingers lingered there. Even through his shirt she could feel the heat from his skin. His whole body was hot and hard, thrumming with tension.

Leaving her bra intact, he pulled back to look at her.

She blinked at him, too dazed to focus or understand what was happening. His breathing came fast and heavy. She felt it as her palms slid from his shoulders down to his chest.

"I assume you have a bed," he murmured, capturing her hands and kissing the backs of her curled fingers.

"Hmm?"

"Honey, it's that or this tile floor. Take your pick."

Some of the haze lifted and she saw the glint of humor in his lust-darkened eyes. "Oh, right." She sucked in a breath, thinking she'd never been with a man like Lucas before and probably never would be again. "Come."

His lips quirked at her stupid word choice, but he said nothing as she took his hand and led him through the living room down the short hall. Earlier she'd made sure her room was tidy, her favorite satiny blue sheets clean. She'd even sprayed them with a touch of vanilla and suddenly hoped she hadn't gone overboard.

They entered her semidark bedroom, the curtains already drawn.

"I haven't seen one of those in a while," he said, glancing at her double bed as he slipped her top button free.

"It's an old house with small rooms. A queen would be nice but impractical." She started with a button in the middle of his chest. "Since I don't usually entertain men here."

"Usually?"

Startled by his slightly mocking tone, she looked up at him.

"I bet your neighbors are all packing heat. Even that tiny white-haired lady on your right."

"Hazel?" Melanie grinned. "Count on it."

"Maybe I should move my truck," he said, searching her face while he freed another button.

"Hazel won't shoot you. Just call the sheriff."

He hesitated. "I'll make sure to leave before dark." His patient smile made her want to cringe.

Now she understood what he'd been getting at about moving his truck. He wanted to know if he'd be spending the night. Sometimes she was so naive it exhausted her. Sighing, she nodded. "Yes, before dark—that would be best."

"Don't look so glum." He nudged her chin up. "That gives us several hours," he murmured, looking into her eyes and pushing the blouse off her shoulders.

She stared back, captivated by his handsome face, his strong hands, his deft touch. His shirt hung open and her gaze moved down to his broad muscled chest. She'd already seen him shirtless and she wanted to see him again. She wanted to know how all that smooth tanned skin felt under her palms and against her lips.

Suddenly she was frantic to strip his shirt off, grabbing the front and trying to push it off him. He caught her wrists, holding both of them in one hand, stilling her, while he unhooked her pink bra. The cups loosened, and his gaze drifted down to her breasts, to nipples already tight and aching for his touch.

For several sizzling seconds, he just looked down at her, his gaze sweeping her collarbones, her breasts, her belly.

"Pink," he murmured with a faint smile, using his thumb to trace the bra's lace scalloping. Then he slid the satiny straps off her shoulders.

She smiled a little herself, wondering how he planned on getting the bra off without releasing her wrists. Turned out he had no trouble at all. Then he went for the zipper on her shorts.

"No fair," she protested, and he completely ignored her. "I mean it." She twisted free of his hold. "Your shirt has to go."

His expression was one of pure amusement. "Yes, ma'am." He shrugged out of his shirt and nodded at the blue handmade quilt covering her bed. "Want that out of the way?"

"What?" She had to quit ogling his chest. "Yes." She folded the coverlet back and glanced around the small room, then ended up putting it in the corner on the floor.

She turned back to Lucas and found him sitting on the edge of the bed pulling off his second boot. His jeans were unsnapped and halfway unzipped. The predatory glint in his eyes made him look dark and dangerous. God help her, it turned her on.

"Take off your shorts." He stood, finished unzipping his jeans and stripped them off.

He still wore black boxers, and she tried to see more of him but he was fishing for something in the pocket of his jeans and blocking her view.

"If you're too busy, I reckon I can do it," he said with a trace of amusement, and she glanced up just as he took a packet out of his wallet.

She felt the heat bloom in her cheeks but she just laughed. So what? She'd caught him staring lots of times. He tossed his jeans aside, and she held her breath while he slid off the boxers.

Oh, my.

"The shorts, Melanie," he said quietly, humor replaced by barely restrained need. "I'd hate to rip them."

In her haste the zipper caught. It snagged a second time as she watched him come toward her. She let go, thinking he'd finish, and if he ripped the shorts—oh, well. Instead he used his hands to cover her bare breasts. His mouth brushed her ear, then the skin below it. He caught her earlobe with his teeth, biting gently, the slight pressure crazily erotic.

She could've sworn he hadn't moved either hand from her breasts, and yet she felt the shorts slide down her legs. In another instant her panties were gone, and he was picking her up and laying her across the bed. Her hair went everywhere, tangling in his fingers and clinging to her cheeks.

He stretched out beside her, his naked body pressed against hers while he lifted the tendrils off her skin. A frown lowered his brows. "Your face is damp."

"Is it?" She wasn't crying, if that was what he thought. "Oh, Lucas, I'm damp all over."

For a second he stared at her, and then he let out a short laugh. Her first instinct was to hide her face against his shoulder. But she refused to give in to something so childish. Lucas made her feel bolder, more powerful, and she was going to revel in it for as long as it lasted. And, oh, how he made her wet.

"Let's see," he whispered, his warm breath bathing her ear one moment, then filling her mouth with a steamy kiss the next. His hand moved down her body, pausing at her breast to toy with a stiff nipple.

His erection was hot against her hip bone, and he skimmed his fingertips over her ribs and down her belly. When he reached the tip of her folds, she squeezed her thighs together.

He broke the kiss and lifted his head. "You don't want me to touch you?"

"I do. But—" she let out a shaky breath "—I want to touch you first."

Wariness flickered in his eyes, quickly followed by a choked laugh. "Go ahead," he said, falling back on his elbows. "But if I tell you to stop, better do it pronto."

She grinned with the heady awareness of how clearly he wanted her. She pushed halfway up and tried not to stare. But it wasn't as if she could *not* look. Her lips parted on a sigh. He was…impressive.

"Jesus," he murmured, grabbing the packet he'd left on the nightstand.

"Wait—"

He sheathed himself before she could lay a finger on him. "Later," he whispered, rolling toward her, the breadth of his shoulders forcing her back to the mattress.

Without warning he slipped a hand between her thighs. She gasped at the intimate brush of his fingers. She knew her body well, and she wasn't just wet; she was slick. Something he'd just learned for himself, she guessed from his groan.

He kissed her long and hard and deep until she couldn't breathe, couldn't keep track of what he was doing. With a start she realized he'd positioned himself between her legs, one hand caressing the inside of her thigh, stroking higher, higher. Until she arched up to meet his hand.

Like flashes of lightning, the sensations started to burst through her body in intermittent strikes. Shimmering pleasurably one second, exploding the next until at last she convulsed against him. He trembled as he entered her, slowly, before the last shock wave faded.

Looming over her, braced by one arm, he touched the side of her face as he sank into her. She felt weak, spent, yet more alive than she'd ever dreamed possible. He partially withdrew, then thrust into her again, deeper. A cry escaped her and she hooked a leg around him, urging him to go on, to ease the pressure that had started building all over again. He found her ankle, and lifting her other leg, he pulled them both around his waist and thrust with a force that brought her off the mattress.

Three more deep thrusts and another climax pulsed into life. Her body arched convulsively, and behind her eyelids, the darkness shimmered with a thousand pricks of white light.

Lucas slowed suddenly, his body shuddering violently on a final thrust. A low harsh groan came from deep in his throat. They were both trembling when he withdrew from her, careful not to crush her as he sagged against her body before rolling onto his back.

"I saw them," she murmured, almost too weak to lay her hand on his heaving chest.

"What, honey?" He stroked her hair. "What did you see?"

"Stars."

11

LYING FLAT ON his back, Lucas finally gained control of his breathing. He put his arm around Melanie and tucked her warm naked body against his side. Sighing, she pressed her cheek to his shoulder and curled into him. His chest tightened. He didn't know why. Probably because the sex had been good. Better than good. Incredible. Too fast, though.

He glanced at the nightstand clock. They had a couple of hours before he had to leave. If not for her damn neighbors he would've liked to stay the night. Not his usual style. He preferred waking up alone, with the windows wide-open—hot or cold outside, it didn't matter.

She lifted her head. Her smile was shy. "We don't have to stay in bed if you don't want to. We can go to the kitchen."

"Is that what you want?"

"No." She hesitated, her lashes fluttering when he swept the hair away from her eyes. "I know you're hungry."

"Is my belly causing a ruckus?"

"A little bit," she said with a soft laugh.

"Don't listen to it." He shifted so that their gazes met. "It's got no manners."

For a long, quiet, crazy moment they just smiled at each other.

He pushed his fingers into her thick brown hair, lightly rubbing her scalp, watching her eyelids droop. She liked having her head massaged. That was one of several discoveries he'd made about her. She liked rubbing her nipples against his chest—something he appreciated—and she loved it when he nibbled her earlobe. He was getting hard again thinking about all the sweet helpless sounds she made when he touched her in the right place.

Lucas brushed his mouth across her cheek to her ear and waited for the soft sigh that would part her lips. When it came, he leaned in to kiss her.

"Wait." She opened her eyes. "I'm going to ask you something," she said, suddenly alert and serious. "And I want you to please be honest."

That was not something a man wanted to hear after making love to a woman.

She bit her lip. "Was I loud?"

For the second time in the span of a minute, Lucas was at a loss. At one point they'd both gotten loud. "Are you kidding?" he asked, deciding to tease her out of fretting about it. "They could hear you at the Sundance."

Her eyes troubled, she jerked her head when he tried to cup her cheek. "I'm serious."

"Melanie." He covered her hand. It was cold and he squeezed gently. "I don't think we made enough noise to worry about. I really don't."

She stared for a moment. Finally her lips lifted in a smile that seemed strained. "I'm sure you're right."

"Look, I know you're a teacher. It's a small town. I get it. But you're allowed to have a life, and the only way your neighbors could've heard was if they'd been listening at their open windows."

"No, you don't get it." She looked so miserable that all he wanted to do was hold her. "You really don't, because

I haven't told you everything. I'm not sure why I'm telling you now."

He sat up, his back against the pillows, then gathered her in his arms. His cock was finally calming down. "I'm listening."

She pulled the sheet up to cover her breasts. "I guess I'm telling you because I don't want you to think I'm being silly or overreacting about protecting my privacy."

"Okay," he said, growing mildly concerned over the tension he felt in her body.

"My father is a minister. He has quite a large congregation, including most of my students." She sighed. "And neighbors."

Speechless yet again, Lucas let the new information trickle through his brain. He had no idea what he'd expected her to say but it wasn't that she was a preacher's daughter. Where he came from, small-town preachers and their families lived in glass houses and were held to strict standards. Man, back in high school, guys knew to stay away from the preacher's daughters…even the wild, rebellious ones who had something to prove.

He flashed back to yesterday, to Gertrude and Pauline and how Melanie spent most of her spare time reaching out to the community. How she hadn't once visited the local bar. It all made sense now.

"Jesus," he muttered, then sent her a look of apology. He glanced down where the sheet gaped, exposing part of her breast, and he pulled his arms away from her. "You do a nice thing like invite me to dinner and here I am taking advantage of you."

She gasped, her eyes widening. "I hope you're joking."

"Are you?"

"No, of course not."

Hell, he didn't think so. "Look, Melanie, if I had known…"

"Stop it." Her tone was angry. "Just stop it," she repeated, more calmly. She let go of the sheet, baring her breasts to him. He cursed himself because he had to look. She was gorgeous. "Thinking you took advantage of me is ridiculous. Was I not a participant?" She'd moved closer, reclaiming the small space he'd put between them. "If I've seemed skittish, it's because I need to be careful, and frankly, before you, I never had to think about it."

She curled a hand around the back of his neck, leaned in to kiss him, her breasts grazing his chest. It was tempting to let the conversation die. Let their bodies do the talking. But he owed it to her to tell her about himself. He doubted his incarceration would ever become public knowledge, but with Shea returning tomorrow and everything still up in the air with Safe Haven, he couldn't be sure. If a deal wasn't struck between the sanctuary and PRN, he didn't want the blame resting on his shoulders. But most of all, he didn't want Melanie hurt.

They both got carried away with the kiss, but when she started to straddle him, he stopped her and steeled himself against her wounded expression.

"Now I have something to tell you," he said, brushing his lips over the frown lines between her brows. "Before we do anything else."

She nodded, watching him with a wariness that made him want to hold her in his arms and lie his ass off. He wouldn't, and not just because this was Melanie. He might be many things but he'd never been a liar.

"I used to go to church with my mother and sister when I was a kid. In fact, I was a regular churchgoer until I was in my twenties. We had two churches outside of town and two preachers. They both had daughters, and everyone seemed to know where they were going, what they were doing and who they were doing it with."

"Lucas, you don't have to worry—"

He put a silencing finger to her lips. "This isn't headed

where you think." His sigh brought the wariness back to her face. "I have a good idea what it's like for you, and there's something you need to know about me. Just in case it comes out." He rubbed her arm. "I'm an ex-con. I was in prison for three years. They released me thirteen months ago."

She seemed surprised but not shocked. The blood hadn't drained from her face; she hadn't leaped off the bed to run and hide or throw up. She hadn't even pulled away. But then, maybe his words still needed to sink in.

"That's why I'm so passionate about the Wild Horse Training Program," he said when she remained silent. "It saved my life."

She blinked. "You trained mustangs."

"Yep. I was involved with the program for the last two years of my sentence. I also taught other inmates how to train the horses." Relief poured through him that she was taking it so well, but he knew she had more processing to do. "I don't usually broadcast that I'm an ex-con. Sometimes I'll mention it if I think it might curb someone's bias about the program."

"I would imagine you'd be a shining example of its success. But I also understand why you wouldn't want to out yourself. People can be horribly nosy and judgmental." Rolling her eyes, she added, "Even churchgoers."

"You're taking this well," he said, studying her calm expression. He reached for her cold hand and found where her nerves were hiding. "You're better off staying away from me. If people hear you've been hanging out with an ex-con, it could be bad for you. Maybe even bad for your family, too. I don't know."

"You paid your debt to society, didn't you?"

"Yep, but for a lot of folks a prison term isn't good enough. They think you should pay for the rest of your life."

She tilted her head. "Did you murder anyone?"

He snorted. "No."

"Steal? Rob a bank?"

He shook his head, wondering where she was going with this.

"Hold someone at gunpoint? Harm a child?"

"No," he said, his patience fraying. Obviously, she wanted to make a point. "And if I'd said yes to any of those things?"

"I wouldn't have believed you." She smiled as if she thought *he* was the one being naive. "If you don't mind my asking, what were you convicted of?"

"Does it matter?"

"It's just...I can't imagine what you could've possibly done to get three years."

"Aggravated assault."

"Were you guilty?"

"The state of Wyoming thought so."

"That's not what I asked."

He released her hand and rubbed his eyes. They were in bed, both naked, having this conversation. Shit. "Technically, yes."

"What exactly happened?" She shifted closer, picking up his arm and putting it around her.

The trusting gesture made his chest tighten. "I told you how I'd bought a ranch and was fixing it up. A month after I moved in, I found out that a man named Cal Jessup had been trying to buy the place for years, just like he'd bought up every other ranch in the area. He'd been feuding over water rights with the previous owner. The old guy probably would've taken twenty bucks from me rather than sell to Jessup.

"He came to me with a sizable offer. Of course, I turned it down, and from that minute on, I became the enemy. I didn't get it right away. He was cordial at first, but when he realized I was there to stay, he started playing dirty.

Little things at first, petty vandalism that cost me time and money I didn't have. Or he'd quibble about property lines, and his lawyers would send me threatening letters." He shrugged. "Most of it I just ignored. And then he went too far."

Lucas briefly closed his eyes, exhaling, forcing some of the tension out of his body. Memories of that terrible day still had the power to anger him if he wasn't careful.

Melanie cupped his face, her soothing touch helping to neutralize the demons. "We don't have to talk about this now," she said softly. "Or ever."

Basking in her gentle smile did the trick. The brutal image faded from his mind. "I want you to know. I need to tell you." Struck by a sudden realization, he started to shut down. Explaining would be selfish. No one wanted to hear this, especially not someone as tenderhearted as Melanie. It was far kinder to let her think what she wanted.

"Lucas?"

"I was wrong about telling you…." He pulled her hand away from his face. "It's not pretty, and there's no way to clean it up." He tried to roll over to get out of bed but she grabbed his arm.

Her frown was as fiercely determined as her smile had been comforting. "I don't need pretty. Life can be messy. Horribly messy. You, of all people, understand that."

Dammit, even at a time like this she could tempt a smile out of him. He wondered how many people witnessed this fearless and dogged side to her. "It would hurt me to explain."

After studying him for a moment, she shook her head. "No, you're trying to spare me. While I appreciate the gesture, I'm not letting you get away with it."

"Melanie," he said with a warning sigh.

"Lucas." She echoed his warning. "Just tell me."

He sat back and stretched his neck to the side, but the

tension wasn't going anywhere. "Jessup and I shared a watering hole that sat on our property line. It was part of a larger spring we both used for watering our animals. That summer was freaking hot, verging on drought conditions, and more and more mustangs were depending on that watering hole."

Rubbing his arm when he paused, she gave him an encouraging smile. He could see her heart in her eyes, not a trace of doubt. She wanted him to unload.

That was about to change. Only thing he could do to ease the ugliness was to not paint too vivid a picture. "I'd been mending fences in the area. They'd been neglected for years and it was taking me a while. For two weeks I passed that watering hole every day until one particular Sunday. The next Monday I rode by and saw a chain-link fence around the whole damn thing. I knew right away it was Jessup. He was always complaining about the mustangs drinking *his* water. I was so pissed off I tried to pull the sucker down.

"But I needed the bolt cutters that I had in the truck. On my way back with them I saw the dead mustang. You could tell he was an old fellow and he'd been trying to get to the water."

Her eyes widened in horror and she clapped a hand to her mouth. He'd left out how he'd known the horse had fought desperately for water. After four years the gruesome scene was still plain as day.

"Jessup should've been the one locked up," she whispered, her eyes moist. "Why you?"

"I had most of the fence down when he and his hired man showed up. I admit, I lost my temper. I was cussing and made some threats about what I'd do if he put the fence back up." Lucas shrugged. "He got in my face and I threw a punch. He went down long enough for me to get ahold of myself. Jessup's twenty years my senior and overweight...."

I didn't want to seriously hurt the guy." He snorted. "Yeah, I did, especially when he got up and kept goading me. But I didn't. I walked away." Surprisingly, he was finding some relief in recounting the story. "I should've wised up when I saw his man standing back with his arms folded, watching me slug his boss."

"They set you up?"

"It was obvious, at least to me. Can't prove it."

"But three years for a single punch?"

"Jessup and his man had a different version." Edgy again, Lucas thought longingly about a cold beer. "It's likely I gave Jessup a black eye or a bloody nose, but he looked a whole lot worse by the time he showed up at the emergency room. Somebody else had tuned him up pretty good. Wish it had been me, but hey."

A brief smile lifted the corners of her lips. "I've never struck a living thing in my life but I think I could've made an exception for him." She sank against the pillows, letting the sheet slip below her breasts. "It had to be his hired hand, and they both lied."

"The real kicker was the bolt cutters and the rifle in my truck. Brought the charge up to aggravated assault."

"What? You didn't threaten him with the bolt cutters," she said, and he shook his head even though she wasn't looking for confirmation. "And every rancher I know keeps a rifle in his truck in case he has to protect his livestock."

"Honey, you're preaching to the choir." Trying to control a smile, he nuzzled the side of her neck. "Ever heard that one before?"

"I don't know how you can joke. Three years of your life. And that poor horse."

"Don't go there." He leaned back to look at her. Misery darkened her eyes. "Dammit, Melanie, that's why I didn't want to tell you. You can't keep thinking about this." He caught her chin and held her still. "Do you understand?"

"But don't you want to just—?"

"No, I don't. I can't. Letting it go is the only way I can find peace." He released her chin, afraid he might be hurting her. "Anger and wanting revenge doesn't help."

"You didn't belong in prison," she whispered. "You were innocent."

She'd never know how much her support meant to him. Before she'd asked about his crime, she'd accepted his prison term as his contrition. Refused to believe him capable of a heinous criminal act. Melanie not only believed in him, but she also accepted him, warts and all.

His throat constricted, playing hell with his ability to swallow.

She looked up when he touched her cheek, and she gave him the sweetest smile.

"So what now?" he asked when he could trust his voice to sound normal. What happened next, tomorrow... It was up to her.

"I say we stick to the plan."

"Refresh my memory."

With a mock glare, she said, "You leave before dark."

"And?"

She laughed, burying her face against his shoulder, her blush warm on his skin. "We stay in bed until then."

Lucas clutched her hair and tilted her head back until he could look into her warm brown eyes. He wasn't trying to embarrass her—she was beautiful when she blushed. But that wasn't the only reason he couldn't look away. He wanted to remember how her eyes hadn't changed after she knew the truth. How she'd accepted him, believed in him.

He lowered his mouth, tasting her sweet generous lips and then her tongue, pleased at her eager response. Bending her knee, she moved her thigh up toward his cock. She stopped short, but he knew it was a logistical problem and not hesitance.

Anyway, he wasn't in a hurry. The loving had happened too quickly the first time. He wanted to use this second chance to do it right, explore every inch of her body and give her pleasure. And if she wanted to stay exactly as they were, he wouldn't mind that, either. It felt good just to hold her.

She broke the kiss and smiled when he tightened his arm around her. "What you said earlier about preferring to keep your past private… It's better you don't say anything." Her gaze flickered. "Yes, for me, but also your program. I'd like to believe no one would judge us—" she sighed "—but we have to be realistic. If the board has to be involved—"

"I know," he said, cutting her off because he could see she didn't want to talk about this, and he didn't, either. "I agree. We keep this to ourselves."

Smiling, she slid her arms around his neck and he held her close. He had to hand it to her—she didn't seem naive about people being hypocrites, even decent God-fearing people. But he didn't care about them. Something else was starting to gnaw at him. He hoped it wasn't shock that had tempered her reaction. When the haze cleared and she was alone with her thoughts, there was no telling how she'd feel tomorrow.

12

THE NEXT AFTERNOON Melanie stood at the office window watching Lucas work on the new corral. Monday was a regularly scheduled day for her and the students to come to Safe Haven, and thank goodness for that. She'd barely made it through morning classes in a coherent state. She doubted that even the sophomore girls were as silly about their dates as she was being, replaying every detail from last night ad nauseam.

Melanie really needed to get a grip. It sure didn't help that he was working without a shirt. But she was an adult, a professional, and she needed to step away from the window. Go back to the desk. Better yet, check on the students working in the barn and quarantine stable, inventorying meds with Kathy. The farther Melanie got away from Lucas, the better. Shea would be arriving in about an hour, and there was still so much to do.

She heard the door open and she guiltily turned around. "David? What are you doing here?"

Dressed in his customary conservative suit and boring tie, his expression noncommittal, her boss glanced around the small office without answering. Not that it mattered. She knew with dreaded certainty that he'd heard she'd had

Lucas over last night. That was the only reason for David to show up like this. He wanted to see for himself if anything was going on.

Finally he decided to give her his attention. He found her waiting with her arms crossed and lifted his brows. She wasn't happy and she didn't care if he knew it. If this was about Lucas, and she couldn't imagine anything but, it was none of David's business.

"I was hoping to talk to you before you left school today," he said. "But apparently you were in a rush."

"You were in a meeting, and I left the same time I always do." It was a tiny, tiny lie. More like a fib. But what was five minutes? "You could've called."

"You don't always answer."

Tempted by sarcasm, she refrained from responding to the subtle reprimand. "Well, you found me. What can I do for you?"

He smiled pleasantly enough before he moved toward the window.

No. Not there.

She tried to swallow but her mouth was suddenly dry. "I assume you came to see what the kids have been doing out here," she said affably. "You should've come earlier for our session on animal husbandry. Right now most of them are helping in the barn and quarantine stable. I'll show you—"

"Do you really think it's proper for that man to be working without a shirt?" he asked, frowning, and boy, did he not want to hear her answer. "After all, you have impressionable teenage girls here under your supervision."

"For heaven's sake, he's practically old enough to be their father," she said with a dismissive wave of her hand. "Besides, the girls aren't working anywhere near him."

The condescending lift of his brow didn't bode well.

Reluctantly, Melanie joined him at the window. "Dammit, Chelsea," she muttered.

Realizing what she'd said, she held her breath. It wasn't anything horrible, but she never used that language. And David knew it. Great. She'd given him something else to blame on Lucas.

She refused to look at David. "Chelsea is not supposed to leave her assigned area. She knows better. I'll go deal with it."

David stopped her from leaving. She met his eyes, then glanced at the hand he'd laid on her arm. "I thought you knew better, as well," he said, his touch turning a bit possessive. "You've done a lot of good work with the students here. If you remember, you met with opposition from some of the parents, but I supported you. You've expressed interest in expanding the program. I can't fathom why you'd want to jeopardize all you've accomplished. Or hope to."

Panic and fear battled with anger inside her. She believed she grasped his meaning but prayed she was wrong. "You're aware of how much I appreciate you going to bat for me." Melanie moved her arm so he had no choice but to release her. "What I don't understand is how Chelsea's minor infraction could endanger a program we both know is invaluable to these kids."

"This isn't about a student's disobedience," he said, studying her with an intense and unnerving curiosity. "If you truly don't understand what's going on, I strongly suggest you give it some thought."

She watched him adjust the knot in his tie, something he did when he was agitated. Perhaps he was trying to decide if she was being deliberately obtuse or whether he should give her the benefit of the doubt. Normally, she could read him more easily.

Other than the reference to the kids' tenuous Safe Haven project, he'd been vague and careful. He'd said nothing about her career or reputation being on the line, nor had he even hinted at the personal relationship he wanted with her. However tempted she was to force him to own up to the veiled threat, one of them had to back down. Unfortunately, she had the most to lose.

Soon Lucas would be gone. She hoped that didn't mean she'd never see him again, but was that realistic? Or just wishful thinking? Or perhaps crazy thinking, considering what he'd told her last night. She felt no differently toward him. If anything, he'd gone up in her estimation. He'd paid a huge price for doing the right thing, for doing what she herself would've done. At least, she wanted to believe she had that kind of courage.

David was being a jerk. But he was right. Her formerly crystal clear future had turned a bit murky. She did have some serious thinking to do. While she wasn't prepared to be a doormat for him or anyone else, she couldn't afford to be reckless, either.

Swallowing her pride, she pasted on a smile. "I appreciate your concern and counsel, and—" she breathed in deeply "—I'll do just that."

His features relaxed. "I'm glad. Truly. You know I have only your best interest at heart."

She managed a small nod. "I'll get Chelsea. Then I'll show you the stables."

"Don't bother. I have to get back to my office. I'll say something to her on my way out."

"I'll walk you to your car," she said quickly, not wanting him anywhere near Lucas.

His gaze lingered on her face, the longing in his expression making her nervous. Then he reached out a hand. "Melanie…"

Her stomach jumped.

The sound of the doorknob had them both turning. It was Shea, and Melanie had never been happier to see her.

"Hey, stranger, you're early."

"Oh, yeah." Shea shrugged, which likely meant she'd gotten the flights mixed up. Brilliant in most areas, she often spaced over the little things. She gave David a brisk smile. "Am I interrupting?"

"No," Melanie said.

David shook his head. "I was on my way out."

Melanie gladly held the door for him. "I'll see you back at school."

"I'll be in meetings the rest of the afternoon."

"Tomorrow, then," Melanie said pleasantly, holding on to a smile while he hesitated. If he thought for one second she'd agree to see him later, he could go suck a lemon.

Finally he nodded at Shea, then left. Melanie closed the door and sighed.

"Your boss, right?"

"Yes. Haven't you met David before?"

Shea frowned. "Maybe."

"It doesn't matter." Melanie rushed to the window when she remembered about Chelsea. And Lucas. David did not need to meet him. "Oh, Jesse's here with you."

He was leaning against a pole talking to Lucas. Chelsea was walking toward the barn with a grumpy expression on her face. Someone had obviously said something to her but it wasn't David. He was headed for his car. God bless Jesse for unwittingly running interference.

"He picked me up at the airstrip," Shea said, coming to stand at the window with her. "You put the PRN guy to work?"

"Not me. Lucas volunteered. He's been helping Levi around here and figured he'd start the new corral while he waited for you." After a brief silence, she tore her gaze away from Lucas and glanced at Shea, who was frowning at her. Melanie cleared her throat. "How was your trip?"

Shea ignored the inane question. "What's that funny look on your face?"

"What look?" Melanie wondered if she meant the touch of extra makeup she'd used this morning. It was only mascara and a tiny bit of blush, certainly nothing Shea, of all people, would notice. "We'll have to discuss this PRN thing as soon as possible since it might require a board vote," she said, moving to the desk and sifting through stacks of paper. She chanced a peek and saw Shea turn her puzzled frown back to the window.

"Oh." Shea sighed. "Now I get it."

"Get what?" Melanie saw the impatience flash in her friend's face. "Okay, okay." She groaned and gave up shuffling invoices. "Lord help me if even *you* can see that I've got my panties in a twist over him," she said, returning to the window.

Shea didn't take offense. She accepted that she was often clueless about this sort of thing. "Now I understand something Jesse said on the way here." In a rare display of physical affection, Shea gave her a solemn one-arm hug. "If it helps, he thinks Lucas has his panties in a twist over you, too."

LUCAS GRABBED HIS T-shirt when he saw the women walking toward him and Jesse. From a distance they almost looked like sisters. They were close to the same height and build, and both had thick dark hair, though Melanie's was a little longer. She also filled out her jeans better. Not that he was biased, he thought with wry amusement as he pulled on his shirt.

He wiped the sweat from his eyes and smiled at Melanie. Now that they were a few feet away, the differences between the women were obvious. Melanie had perfect lips, a perfect smile and beautiful, intelligent brown eyes that made more than his brain perk up.

No disrespect to Shea.

Melanie and Jesse both tried to introduce her at the same time. Then simultaneously backed off. Without missing a beat, Shea ended up finishing the introduction, which she punctuated with a no-nonsense handshake. He'd been warned about her direct manner. Didn't bother him. It was the intimate way Jesse was gazing at her that unsettled Lucas.

Made him feel a little jealous and a whole lot foolish. Jesse and Shea had an honest committed relationship. There was no chance for anything like that with Melanie. They could share their bodies and a few confidences. Build some memories. But that was it.

"I appreciate you being understanding about my unexpected trip," Shea said, putting her hand up to shade her gray-blue eyes. "Mel emailed me a summary of what you're looking to accomplish. I read it on the plane, but unfortunately, we have to ask for more of your patience. The board might have to vote."

"No problem," Lucas said. "I have time. A week, anyway."

Jesse rubbed Shea's back and used his body to protect her from the sun. "Honey, it's hot, and I know you must be tired. What do you say the four of us have dinner tonight and we talk then?" He waited for her nod, then raised a questioning brow at Melanie and Lucas. "Okay with you guys?"

Not so much. Lucas had hoped to spend the evening with Melanie. Alone. But maybe that was never meant to be, since she refused to look at him. It gave him a bad feeling even though they'd talked earlier.

"Okay with me," he said, and she finally glanced at him.

Her shoulders stiffened. Addressing Jesse and Shea, she murmured, "I think that'll be all right. I need to check my calendar at school to be sure. Where are you thinking of going, Marge's?"

Time in prison taught a guy real quick how to read body language. She sounded deceptively calm, her tone almost matching her expressionless face. But she'd made two unsuccessful attempts to swallow, and she was trying too hard to keep her gaze from wavering. He'd bet her thoughts were bouncing all over the map.

"The diner's okay." Jesse shrugged. "If we eat on the later side, we'll minimize interruptions. The Sundance is the other option. There's always enough food for an army."

"Oh, right, because we'd never be interrupted there," Shea said with a sigh of total exasperation.

Jesse chuckled. "I'm not suggesting we sit with the general population," he said, and Melanie and Lucas exchanged looks at his use of a term typically regarded as prison vernacular. "We can eat in the study or wait until the guests take off for the evening."

Melanie noisily cleared her throat. "The Sundance would probably be best. I'd offer my place but I don't have time to cook." She blinked. "I do have pot roast, if no one cares that it's leftover," she said, then looked directly at Lucas and blushed furiously.

Hell, even he had trouble not reacting. "Whatever you want is fine by me, but let's decide. It's damn hot out here."

"I agree." Melanie fanned her rosy cheeks. "Can you believe it's September?"

"You know what…." Jesse had obviously caught on, judging by the barely suppressed humor in his eyes. "Shea, you're tired. It's not a good night for dinner. And anyway, somebody should probably call Annie and Tucker for their input. We'll get together another night and have a drink, shoot the breeze."

"That works for me," Melanie said, no mistaking the relief in her voice.

Lucas nodded. "Yeah, I'm a little tired myself."

Shea sighed. "Okay, back to square one. I have the bylaws on my computer and a hard copy at home. I didn't want them lost when we moved offices. I'll look them over tonight to see if we need a board vote. Mel, you mind calling Annie?"

"I should have thought to do that already. I'm sorry."

"Hopefully, you were too busy," Shea said in a stage whisper, looking pleased with herself.

Everyone just stared at her for a moment.

Jesse let out a bark of laughter. "Come on, sweetheart. We're going home." Looping an arm around her, he steered her toward the parking lot, stopping her protest with a kiss.

Melanie watched in silence as the couple climbed into Jesse's truck.

"Something wrong?" Lucas asked, wondering if the guy in the suit had anything to do with her edgy mood.

"Nothing I can't handle." She glanced toward the barn. "Chelsea is going to get an earful, that's for sure." She turned back to him. "I hate to ask you this, but could you please work with your shirt on?"

"Right. I wasn't thinking." He felt like an idiot. Normally, he had better manners. But he knew in his gut something else was going on. "Nothing happened with Chelsea. She's a kid. That's how I think of her, so it didn't cross my—"

"Oh, no. No." Melanie didn't just touch his arm; she let her fingers trail down to his hand before she realized what she was doing and abruptly drew back. "It has nothing to do with you. Chelsea knows she's supposed to stick to her assigned area and that's why I'm annoyed with her." A small smile tugged at her mouth. "Personally, I'd prefer you work with nothing on," she said and started laughing before she got out the last word.

Relieved but also frustrated because he couldn't kiss her,

Lucas grinned. “Feeling brave, aren’t you? Think I won’t grab you? No one’s around to see.”

Her eyes widened and she took a step back. “You can’t.” She relaxed when she saw he was teasing. “The man who was here earlier—he’s the principal and my boss. David didn’t like it that Chelsea was talking to you.”

Lucas could understand the man’s concern, given that Chelsea was a shameless flirt. “Does he come out here often?”

“First time.”

“You think it has something to do with me being over at your place?”

“I’d like to say no, but…” She shrugged. “Probably. I’m really not sure.”

Yeah, she was, but she didn’t want to discuss it. “You acted funny about having dinner with Jesse and Shea. Your boss have anything to do with that?”

She blinked and looked back toward the barn. He knew she was stalling, which made him itchy.

“Or maybe it’s about what I told you last night,” he said, and she whipped her gaze to him. “I figured it would take time to sink in, so I get it if you’re uncomfortable now that you’ve considered what it might mean to be associated with me.”

Her mouth dropped open. “Was I surprised? Oh, yeah. Shocked?” She thought for a moment. “Yes, probably shocked. But then you explained the circumstances, so the prison part didn’t change anything for me. If you’d left that fence up, different story. I would think you were a horrible human being. I hate that you have a criminal record because it can haunt you forever.” She smiled gently. “If you let it. But you’re a good man. That’s what counts.”

The ground seemed to shift under his feet. He felt funny, light-headed, probably from the heat. Damn, but September in northern Montana wasn’t supposed to be this hot.

He pulled up the hem of his T-shirt and wiped his moist face. Made extra sure he got the sweat out of his eyes.

When he finally looked at her again, her soft gaze and gentle smile hadn't wavered. He realized right then how much he'd needed to hear her say that. She didn't just understand; she thought he was a good man. The words wouldn't have meant half as much coming from anyone else. Not even from his ex-fiancée.

He'd known Peggy for half his life that day he'd gotten down on one knee and pulled out the ring. She'd been bursting with happiness; so had he. But that was not what he tended to remember when he thought of her. Mostly he recalled that terrible day a month into his sentence. He'd waited and waited for her, holding on to hope until the last possible moment, when he knew with grim certainty she wouldn't be visiting him that day, and she never would again. It wasn't her fault. He'd told her not to wait, to move on. He just hadn't expected her to do it so quickly.

"Lucas?" Melanie had moved closer. She had the sweetest expression on her face. "You seem far away."

It took every ounce of willpower he possessed not to pull her into his arms. She was naive to think he had the power over whether his criminal record would haunt him or not. The cold hard fact was that his record barred him from holding certain jobs or even keeping a rifle. The list didn't end there. But she believed in him, thought he was a good man, and that was something.

"Can we get back to tonight?" he asked, relieved his voice held. "Will I get to see you?"

She exhaled on a quiet sigh, and she looked like a kid who'd had her favorite toy taken away.

"Hey, no pressure." He shrugged. "I know you're busy."

"Shut up."

"What did you say?" He laughed, expecting neither her exasperated tone nor her choice of words.

"Busy has nothing to do with it. You know darn well I want to see you, too."

"So is that going to happen?" he asked, watching her nibble at her lip, tormenting him. "Better tell me quick. You can't expect me to stand this close and keep my hands to myself."

"Oh, no." She hid a smile behind her fingers and moved backward. "Let me figure it out and I'll call you later."

"I was joking. You don't have to go."

"I do. Really, I do. You forget I'm on the clock."

"Look out." He gestured to the post she was about to back into, and she sidestepped it. He smiled. "Just remember, we don't want to disappoint Shea."

Melanie pressed her lips together, laughed anyway and blushed like crazy. She did an abrupt about-face and hurried toward the office.

He watched her cute little butt until she disappeared from view. Still smiling, he picked up the hammer. Alone again with his thoughts, he felt his mood start to backslide.

Man, he hoped he wasn't giving her the wrong impression. He was only working on the corral because Levi had mentioned they needed another one and Lucas had the time. Even his work with PRN was about giving back. He wasn't a do-gooder like Melanie. Maybe she thought too much of him. That would be risky for both of them. He hadn't had someone so firmly in his corner for a long, long time, and it would be foolish for him to get used to it. If he hung around a small town like this, his past was bound to catch up with him and she'd be caught in the cross fire.

Hell, of all the women in northern Montana, it had to be her.... What a pair they made...the sinner and the saint.

13

MELANIE WAS ABOUT to call Lucas when she saw his truck. She'd been sitting in her car in the Safe Haven lot waiting with her door open. If she weren't so anxious to see him and being juvenile about it, she could've used the time to clear some paperwork. But the air had cooled considerably, and after she'd finished feeding the goats and chickens, she'd decided it was too nice to be indoors.

He parked next to her and got out, pocketing his keys and eyeing the small white pickup on the other side of the lot. "We're not alone, I take it."

"No. But Harold is way over in the quarantine stable and he's hard of hearing."

Lucas smiled. "But can he see?"

"Yes, so stop right there." This was so nuts. She felt as if she were back in high school. Or how she imagined she would've felt if she'd actually had a boyfriend to sneak off with. She wished she had the guts to be open about Lucas, but he wasn't a forever guy and she had a responsibility to her parents and her students.

"So how is this thing gonna work?"

"This thing?"

"Yeah," he said, shoving his hands deep into his pockets. "Me not being allowed to touch you or kiss you."

"Hmm." She got out of the car, which put her about five feet away from him. "You know any dirty talk?"

His right brow shot up. "You first."

She grinned. "I thought you were going to wait here for me."

"I wanted to grab a shower." He had on clean jeans, not so faded as the earlier pair, and she liked the snug fit of his collared shirt. The dark blue brought out the color of his eyes, though he needed no help there.

"Let's go to the office," she said, almost afraid to turn her back on him. In high school if a boy had looked at her the way Lucas was looking at her, she would've fainted. She still might.

"I should warn you," he murmured, his voice dropping a notch. "I'm liking the dirty-talk idea a whole lot."

"Um…no." She was inclined to agree, except she'd embarrass herself. And they had business to discuss. "Bad news. I talked to Annie, the former director, and she thinks the board will have to vote."

"Bad news because you know we'll meet with opposition?"

"Not necessarily." She saw that she'd worried him. The truth was, she was concerned after talking to Harold. He'd spoken to Abe, a board member, and the variety-store owner flat out said he wanted nothing to do with the prison system. "The only reason we have a board is so we qualify for government grants. Personally, I wouldn't have chosen the same bunch. Most of them don't really care what happens out here, but if one member is at odds with another over something silly, they can be petty."

"Well, that could be a problem."

She opened the office door. The AC was off but the window was open, so it was pleasant inside. A cool breeze carried in the snorting sounds of the two roans playing in the corral. "We can get around that sort of stuff. It just takes a little more time. Annie and Shea will make a few subtle threats and the bellyachers will heel."

"What about you? Too soft to make threats?" he asked, his voice close to her ear.

In an instant the door was closed behind them and he'd pulled her into his arms.

Melanie leaned into him. "No one takes me seriously," she murmured, letting her head fall back farther with each brush of his lips across hers.

"I do."

"You're sweet-talking me because you want my vote."

"I want *you,*" he whispered and proved it with an urgent kiss as he pulled her tight against him.

She put her arms around his neck, clinging to him, blotting out thoughts of where she was and reasons why she shouldn't be kissing him back. His lips were damp and warm, and the skin at the back of his neck was hot. His arousal pressed against her belly seemed to sear her through the thick denim.

If she didn't stop this, she would burn up. There'd be nothing left of her but ashes and decades of sad tales of the poor disgraced preacher's daughter. And yet all that mattered at this moment was his hungry mouth on hers and the unmistakable need straining his fly.

Her phone buzzed, and they both ignored it.

He lifted her, moving her backward to the desk, shoving the stacks of paperwork to the side. An alarm went off in her head. They'd started something they couldn't finish, not here. And then Lucas yanked her shirt free from the waistband of her jeans and slid his hands underneath, and the tingling sensation of him cupping her breasts through the bra erased all thought.

Melanie clawed at his polo shirt, struggling to pull it up,

wanting so badly to feel skin against skin. Her desperation thwarted her and she fumbled, breathless and frustrated. Lucas eased back a little—she thought to help her—but he gentled the kiss and stilled her hands.

"Lady, I don't know what you do to me," he said softly, resting his forehead against hers. "I don't get carried away like this." He stopped to catch his breath, and she fought for hers, his words turning her on as much as his hard body. "I'm sorry. I know better."

"Screw that," she said weakly, making another attempt to burrow under his shirt.

His laugh sounded rusty. He lifted his forehead from hers and forcefully removed her hands from him. "Don't make it worse. I'm trying to be sensible, dammit."

"We can lock the door." She sounded like a ten-year-old whining to stay up late. That should have shamed her into keeping her hands to herself. "Harold never comes to the office."

"And if someone pulled into the lot?"

"We'd hear the car."

"Would you?"

Slumping back, she let out a sigh, and Lucas sighed along with her.

"I know I wouldn't," he said. His darkened gaze met and held her eyes, almost daring her to look away. "There is nothing I want more than to be inside of you right now."

Her heart lurched.

"But not here. Not anywhere someone could see us. I won't leave you vulnerable to that kind of gossip." He lowered his hand to his side. "Which means I shouldn't touch you, period."

"Why not?" She hooked her fingers behind his belt to keep him from backing up.

"Because I obviously can't trust myself around you."

He lifted her off the desk, holding her only long enough for her to plant her feet on the laminate floor.

"Does that mean no kissing, either?" she said, trying to look innocent.

He snorted a laugh, eyeing her as if she might pounce at any second. "Your father must've had his hands full with you."

"Nothing could be further from the truth." Melanie chuckled at the ridiculous thought. Then she caught sight of the volunteer board. Lucas was right. This was Safe Haven, for heaven's sake. "Apparently I have a problem behaving myself around you, too."

She should've been thanking him for stopping them from doing something foolish, she thought as she turned to straighten the desk. So why did this seem like a punishment and not the sensible thing to do? Maybe because she was tired of being the good girl who never disappointed anyone…except herself.

No matter what, she should feel elated. She, Melanie Knowles, made a hot guy like Lucas lose his head. Wow.

So why didn't she simply invite him back to her house? By tomorrow the whole town would know he'd visited her two nights in a row. Tongues would wag, but there'd be no proof anything untoward happened. People gossiped about things that had no basis in truth all the time. The rumors eventually died. Besides, most folks wouldn't believe her capable of wrongdoing. Wasn't she a paragon of virtue, the perfect sainted extension of her mother?

The thought rankled.

"You know what?" She turned to face him. "Let's go to my house."

Lucas frowned. "You think that's a good idea?"

"Why not? We'd have privacy. I'm entitled to that, right?"

He should've been glad, eager—he shouldn't have

looked troubled. "Melanie, we both know that would be a mistake."

"Why? Did you change your mind about wanting me?"

"No." He kind of laughed, but not at her. Something else was going on inside his head, something that seemed to be pulling him in two different directions. "Was that a text or a call you got?" he asked.

"When?"

"A few minutes ago. It might have to do with PRN and Safe Haven."

She vaguely remembered her phone ringing and dug it out of her pocket. "Huh. One of each." Her breath came out in a whoosh when she saw the call was from David. That would definitely have to wait. The text was from Shea. Melanie read it quickly and looked up with dismay. "We need a vote, so we have to call the members tonight to figure out when everyone can meet."

"We?"

"Me," she said, shrugging. "I won't dump any of it on Shea, since she just got home. I have everyone's phone number at the house. The sooner I get ahold of them, the quicker we can come to terms. I'm sure you're anxious to finish up. You can't be hanging around here forever." She held her breath, waiting for a trace of regret in his eyes or a word of denial—even a token one would do.

At his absent nod, her hope dissolved. "I'll follow you back to town," he said, moving toward the door. "Anything I can do to help?"

She wondered if he'd already discarded her suggestion to go home with her or if he'd considered it at all. Of course, his priority was PRN, not her. She knew that. And if she wasn't wrong about him, Lucas would naturally be trying to protect her from cruel gossip. And if she was wrong…then he'd played her like a fiddle.

No. Not Lucas. She refused to believe that.

"I can't think of anything," she said with a bright smile. "With any luck, we can get them to meet tomorrow."

"That would be great."

He hadn't even tossed her a crumb. And what a fool she was, still hoping for one.

THE BOARD MEMBERS agreed to meet the next afternoon. Melanie should've known twisting arms would be unnecessary. Everyone was curious, anxious to hear more about what Lucas wanted and to see the man himself. Of course they'd requested he be in attendance. She really should've seen that coming, as well. But she hadn't, more evidence that she was off her game. She'd been a little nuts ever since she rammed Lucas's bumper.

The closest spot available for Blackfoot Falls' version of a town hall was a block away. Normally, they'd have met at the Watering Hole, but the earliest the board could gather was after the bar opened.

Seeing the unusual number of cars and trucks parked along Main Street cranked up her grumpiness. The meeting was supposed to be open to members only. Wouldn't surprise her if they'd brought friends, relatives and picnic baskets. That was the trouble with using a public venue. Folks assumed they had a right to barge in anytime.

She walked into the room, and Shea came in seconds behind her. "Who are all these people? Are we in the wrong place?"

Jesse had followed Shea inside. With a wry smile, he placed his hands on her shoulders. "No. This is one of those small-town things we talked about," he said. "So don't bite anyone's head off. Okay?"

"I'd never do that." The sly wink she gave Melanie nearly bowled her over.

Jesse just smiled.

"Seriously," Shea said, twisting around to look at both of them. "Can't we kick these people out?"

Louise from the fabric shop was passing by and obviously overheard. She gave Shea a chilly glare that Shea completely ignored, probably hadn't even noticed.

"It's 4:28." Jesse nodded at the head table facing the room of thirty-something people. "Go get 'em, tiger."

Melanie knew Lucas wasn't there yet—she'd already surveyed the room. They'd decided it was best not to come together, but she'd expected him to be here by now. She ordered herself not to fret and followed Shea. Four other board members were already seated at the second table, which formed an L. After Lucas and the rest of the board showed up, she'd suggest to Jesse that they lock the doors. Latecomers would gripe, but too bad.

Leaving two places for Jesse and Lucas between her and Shea, Melanie set down her notebook and pulled out a chair. Still edgy, she checked her phone to make sure she hadn't missed a text from Lucas, then glanced up and saw him standing by the door, looking at her. Her smile was automatic.

It died the second she spotted David entering the building. With purpose in his stride, he headed directly for a seat in the front row. Okay, now it was time to fret.

"I SAY WE hear from this Lucas fella himself," someone called out from the audience.

Melanie thought it sounded like Earl Lester, but she couldn't be sure. Not that she cared. They were half an hour into a meeting that should've taken five minutes. Partly because Shea had stuck to the format described in the bylaws, up to and including reading the minutes of their last meeting. Shea could be anal at times, but Melanie suspected she was trying to bore the heck out of everyone so they'd leave. Good plan…in theory. No one had budged, including David.

He sat patiently listening to everything being said, careful not to show particular interest in Melanie or Lucas. Did he think she was an idiot? He had no reason to be here. But if challenged, he'd probably use her student project to justify his involvement.

Shea scanned the audience. "Will the person who just spoke please stand and identify himself?"

No one responded, so Shea sat back and waited. After a few moments of cranky mumblings among the crowd, Earl got to his feet. The stoop in his spine had less to do with age than a back injury he'd sustained thwarting a pair of drifters who'd tried to rob his filling station. No surprise he sat on the opposing team.

"I'm Earl Lester, and I say we let Mr. Sloan tell us in his own words why we should give a damn about a bunch of no-good bottom-feeders. They sure ain't behind bars for being model citizens," he said, buoyed by supportive murmurs. "Let 'em all rot in their cells."

Melanie slid a discreet glance at Lucas. His calm expression remained unchanged. He hadn't moved so much as an eyelash. She wanted to respond to Earl, remind the whole audience the prisoners had already been judged, remind them of their Christian duty to forgive. But she couldn't, not with David sitting there. He'd assume anything she said would have more to do with her personal feelings toward Lucas than the program itself.

"Everyone be quiet," Shea said, and she didn't have to raise her voice. "Mr. Lester, with all due respect, you're not a member of this board. You're not even a volunteer…. Correct me if I'm wrong." She paused, her gaze direct and unwavering. "So what you have to say is irrelevant. Oh, and very annoying."

Jesse let out a laugh that he tried to cover with a short

cough. Sadie and Will, sitting with the rest of the board members at the other table, made no attempt to hide their laughter. Some in the audience expressed amusement, but mostly Shea's words were met with stunned silence or indignant stares.

Earl flushed deep red.

Jesse reached under the table and squeezed Shea's thigh. "He doesn't mean any harm," he whispered to her, and then he said, "Earl, she's right. I don't know why all you folks are here. Safe Haven doesn't concern any of you. That being said, we've all witnessed what can happen to unwanted animals. We're very fortunate to not only have the sanctuary in our community but have it run by capable, selfless people. They care about the animals. That's what this is about."

After a few moments of blessed silence, Lucas turned to Jesse and Shea. "If you don't mind, I'd like to speak to the gentleman's question."

Jesse looked to Shea and she nodded.

Lucas got up, and Melanie's heart pounded so hard it hurt. She should've expected this. Now she could only hope he knew what he was doing.

"Can everyone hear me?" he asked and got quite a few encouraging nods. He'd wisely dressed in clean work jeans, a dark blue T-shirt and scuffed boots, looking no different from any cowboy shopping at the Food Mart or cashing his paycheck at the bank.

Melanie chanced a peek at David, saw he was watching her and pretended to look at someone beyond him.

"I can appreciate why you folks might be hesitant," Lucas said, his empathetic smile a perfect combination of understanding and concern. "And to be frank, I'm glad you have qualms and that you're willing to ask questions. We all need to give voice to animals who can't speak for themselves. That's part of the reason I'm here."

He'd also shaved again. His jaw and chin were smooth, and though she missed the sexy stubble that gave him a slightly dangerous quality, she knew presenting this clean-cut image was smart.

"I'm grateful for this opportunity to help you understand how the program works and how it benefits the horses, inmates and society in general." He seemed comfortable, easily making eye contact with the audience.

Some sour expressions began to fade. The women up front sat straight and attentive, smiles on their lips as they waited for him to go on.

"First, I'll flat out give you my word that any horse that goes into the program, no matter if it's a stray, mustang or has been abandoned, is well cared for. The horse is examined by a vet, trimmed, vaccinated and, if need be, gelded."

"That's all well and good," Earl called out. "But you can't give us your word that they won't be mistreated by those other animals in jail."

Melanie tensed, watching for Lucas's reaction.

He stayed calm and even gave an understanding nod. "The men aren't randomly chosen to work with the horses. They're vetted ahead of time by case workers to determine suitable candidates. And of course, they're closely supervised."

"Men?" Earl packed the single word with sarcasm. "Don't sugarcoat it, son. You mean vermin."

The sound of a fist pounding wood echoed off the walls.

Everyone turned to Sadie, who was glaring at Earl. "Shut your fool mouth and let him finish. I gotta get back to the Watering Hole. Some of us have businesses to run." She turned to Lucas, and her glare instantly softened to a smile. Even a woman old enough to be his mother wasn't immune to those blue eyes. "Go on."

Lucas gave Sadie her very own smile, making her cheeks a little pink, and Abe, sitting next to her, scowled. Everyone knew he had a "secret" thing for her. After what Harold had told Melanie, Abe was the board member with whom she was most concerned. She knew which way his vote would go.

"All right," Lucas said genially, making sure his gaze touched everyone. He even managed to include Melanie for what seemed like a long private moment. "Since we're at a break, any other questions before I continue?"

She had no idea how the people in the audience responded. She couldn't drag her attention away from him. He was good at this—really good, she thought—and she didn't know why it bothered her.

14

LUCAS KNEW IT was a mistake the moment he'd opened the floor to questions. It was too early. Normally, his timing was better. But then he'd looked at Melanie, remembered how much was at stake and lost his game. He'd never wanted to win over a crowd more than he did today. For several reasons, most of them crazy.

Ten minutes and three pointless questions later, he finally regained control. He used the last query regarding funding to get back on track. "There are no out-of-pocket expenses for any participating sanctuaries or for taxpayers," he said. "Once the horses go through a four-month training period, they're put up for adoption or sold at auction, which funds the program. Either way, what's important is that we know where these horses end up, and it's not a slaughterhouse or glue factory.

"By the way, horses aren't the only animals in the program. Prison farms produce everything from beef and dairy cattle to goats and water buffalo, and a few even train service dogs." Most of the listeners seemed surprised, some impressed, both common reactions. Lucas got an unexpected glimpse of David Mills. He looked as if he was picturing Lucas with a rope around his neck.

Before he could move on, David stood.

"Pardon me," he said, very polite, very authoritative. And unfortunately, the crowd seemed eager to hear from him. "I'd like to address an earlier comment you made about the benefits of the program for prisoners and society alike. I understand why the inmates would welcome the chance to break the monotony of their daily grind." He hadn't been so crass as to question why anyone should care—his tone and faint smirk were implication enough. "How does society benefit?"

"I'm glad you asked." Lucas could feel Melanie's tension from six feet away. That alone was enough to make him dislike the guy, though Lucas had a couple more reasons. "Studies have shown that programs using animals lower recidivism rates. Working with the animals also helps teach inmates compassion and provides them with both work and life skills. In training the horses, a man develops a sense of pride and learns about self-satisfaction. After he does his time and rejoins society, he's a different person." Lucas smiled. "I know that must seem obvious to an educated man like yourself, so if it's statistics you're looking for, I can dig up some."

David's features briefly tightened at the subtle jab. "I would appreciate that," he said. "I'm sure you can understand my concern as the high school principal, considering a number of our students are rather heavily involved with Safe Haven."

Which had nothing to do with the fostered horses being trained hundreds of miles away, but the stupid bastard already knew that. Or maybe not so stupid. The disgruntled mumblings started up again. Score one for David.

"I do," Lucas said. "I completely understand. In fact, to put your mind at ease, I have a proposal. I believe we all agree that giving this program appropriate consideration is the charitable, as well as the right, thing to do. Am I wrong?"

David hesitated, his eyes narrowing a fraction. "Go on."

"Wilcox Prison in Wyoming is a seven-hour drive from here. They're a minimum-security facility that happens to use an animal-assisted program similar to Wyoming State Honor Farm in Riverton. I can give the warden a call. I bet he'd be happy to show off their success." He turned, briefly met Melanie's wide panicked eyes, then went on to Shea. "If Ms. Knowles or Ms. Monroe would care to accompany me to see the program in action, I'm sure we can put everyone's fears to rest."

A stunned silence settled over the room, and Lucas knew he'd gone too far. He only hoped he hadn't pissed off Melanie. At least he'd thought fast enough to include Shea as an option.

"Melanie has classes all week," David said with a slight smugness. "So taking her is out of the question."

Lucas smiled to himself. Did this guy even *know* Melanie? She wouldn't put up with that sort of high-handedness.

"Would the weekend work?" she asked, the barest hint of defiance in her voice. "There's no school this Friday, so I'd be free to leave in the morning."

"Fine with me." Lucas kept his face expressionless as he looked at her. She might have been a little annoyed with him, but he saw the excitement dancing in her eyes. He felt it, too. "I'll make the call."

David surged to his feet. "Now, just a minute—"

Shea stood at the same time, ignoring him and addressing the board members. "Let's go through the motion and take a vote. Any yeses?" Five hands went up. "Are the rest of you opposed or are you maybes?" There were a couple of shrugs and nervous glances cast at the spectators. "Since we're at a stalemate and have nothing more to discuss until Melanie reports back," Shea said, closing her laptop, "this meeting is adjourned."

MELANIE HADN'T EVEN made it through the tuna sandwich she'd hastily slapped together after the meeting when her phone rang. She saw that it was her father and wondered why it had taken him so long.

"Hello, Dad," she said, pushing aside her dinner, her appetite already gone.

"Am I disturbing you?" It was a question he never asked, but then, she always made time for him. "Do you have a moment?"

"Sure."

"Are you at home?"

"I'm sitting at my kitchen table facing stacks of quizzes to be graded. Why?"

He hesitated. "So you're alone?"

She sighed. "Yes." Any number of people could've called him, even someone who hadn't attended the meeting. Her money was on David. She'd just bet he'd hit speed dial before he made it to his car. "I know why you're calling."

"Yes," he said quietly. "I suppose you would."

"Though there shouldn't be any problem. I'll proofread your sermon before I leave on Friday." She bit her lip, feeling guilty for being cheeky. This wasn't easy for him, and he was acting only out of concern for her. David might deserve her petulance, but her father didn't.

"Frankly, I hadn't given it a thought. That isn't why I'm calling."

"Surely you're not worried about me going out of town."

"I'm your father," he said. "Of course I'm worried."

"Oh, Dad…I'll be fine. I'm barely leaving the state," she said with a breezy laugh that was met with heavy silence.

"How much do you know about—?"

"PRN?" She'd deliberately cut him off, hoping to control the conversation. If she gave him a toehold, she'd end up doing exactly what he and everyone else wanted her to do. "Prison Reform Now is a terrific organization. The wild-horse program in particular is impressive, a real win-win for both Safe Haven and the prison system. I'd love to tell you more about it when we have the time."

"I've already looked the program up online."

"Oh." That, she hadn't expected. "So you know what a wonderful cause it is," she said cautiously, praying that he'd found nothing on Lucas.

"Yes, I'm inclined to agree. However, accompanying a strange man, no matter what his affiliation with PRN, on an overnight trip is something else altogether."

She sank back against the chair with relief. "I've gotten to know Lucas a little. In fact, I had him over here for dinner the other night." Of course, her father knew, but it would help to show she wasn't trying to hide anything from him. "He's very dedicated and passionate about the program. He loves animals, and he's even been working on the new corral while he waited for the board to vote."

"Melanie." Her father sighed, and she could picture him removing his horn-rimmed glasses to rub his weary eyes. He was always tired, always giving 150 percent to his congregation. "You're being…rash."

"Do you know me to be a rash person?"

"Generally, no. That's what worries me."

A snide remark nearly made it past her lips. She'd only feel awful later, and stepping out of character would serve no purpose but to justify her dad's concern. "I'm sorry that's the case. I am. But I've made up my mind. We're leaving Friday morning."

"You know people will talk."

"They always do." She sighed. "Out of curiosity, who called you?"

"A couple of people, actually…."

"David Mills?"

He hesitated. "Yes."

"Didn't you wonder why he's sticking his nose into my business?"

"Melanie, he's your boss and wants to protect your reputation. Surely you know he has your best interest at heart. David's a good man."

"Yes, he's a perfectly nice man. But he wants to be more than my boss."

"Would that be so terrible?" he asked quietly. "He's intelligent, well respected and fits right into the community, not to mention the congregation."

The dreadful thought of spending her life with David had her clenching her teeth to keep from saying something she'd regret. It wasn't personal. She'd meant what she'd said—David was a perfectly nice man, generally speaking. But he bored her. More so now that she'd met Lucas. Heaven help her.

The smothering silence was beginning to make her a bit queasy.

"Dad, I have to go. I've got a lot to do before I leave on Friday. Email me your sermon, though. I'll have time for it."

His sigh was heartfelt. "There's no changing your mind?"

"I'll be fine. I promise," she said and with an eerie calm accepted the fact that she'd just lied to her father. Deep down she knew she'd never be the same again. Lucas had ruined her for any other man. And in the end, he was going to break her heart.

MELANIE WOKE WITH a start. She saw a sign for an upcoming exit and tried to blink away the haze of sleep distorting her vision. "Where are we?" she asked, trying to smother a yawn.

Lucas looked over at her and smiled. "About eighty

miles from Wilcox. We ran into some road construction that put us behind. Did you have a nice nap?"

"That would mean I slept for two hours."

"Two hours and twenty minutes."

"Wow. Sorry."

"Don't be." He reached over and rubbed her shoulder. "You needed the rest."

He was a good driver, his late-model truck a smooth ride. After three late nights trying to get caught up with schoolwork and church tasks, Melanie shouldn't have been surprised she'd dozed off.

Finally able to wade through the sleep-induced fog, she smiled back at him. She couldn't see his eyes, since he was wearing sunglasses. But she knew they looked even more blue against his tanned face. "You probably need it more than I do after working so hard on the corral this week."

"Not me. After a day of manual work I sleep like the dead."

She sighed. "That sounds heavenly."

"You have this weekend to catch up, and no one to bother you."

Melanie eyed him, hoping he was trying to be funny. "Really? No one?"

"Don't get me wrong." A lazy arrogant smile curved his mouth. "I'm planning to do all sorts of wicked things to you. Now, will you be bothered by it? I hope not."

A shiver of anticipation rippled through her. "Very sure of yourself, aren't you?"

"Well, hell, we've had three days of foreplay."

She laughed. "Um, sorry, but I think I missed the best part."

"You have any idea how hard it's been watching you prance around Safe Haven with your band of delinquents and me having to keep my hands to myself?"

"I do not prance. And my students aren't—" She studied his profile. "Was it really hard?"

His lips twitched. "Yes, on both counts."

"Oh." She grinned. "Good." She felt a moment's guilt. This was supposed to be a business trip. Or so she'd assured half the population of Blackfoot Falls. Everyone seemed to have an opinion, even folks she saw only once in a while at the Food Mart.

"We were right to keep our distance the last two days," he said. "Didn't make it any easier."

"I know." Twice she'd gone as far as hitting speed dial, dying for him to meet her someplace. She'd disconnected before the first ring. After her father's phone call and David's cool treatment at work, it would've been foolish to press her luck. She glanced at the dashboard clock. "If we're running behind, we'll miss our appointment with the warden."

"I talked to him an hour ago. He'd heard about the new construction, so he figured we'd be held up. We're meeting him at eight in the morning. I hope that's okay. He's doing us a favor by coming in on a Saturday."

"Sure. We can still head back to Blackfoot Falls afterward."

For a moment he said nothing. "If that's what you want."

She held back a smile. "That way we can break up the drive and maybe spend the night halfway."

He slowly turned his head, raising a brow at her. "You're messing with the wrong guy."

"What?" A giggle undercut her attempt to play innocent.

"I'll pull off at the next exit and show you what."

Melanie shivered at the raspy dip in his voice. "We can't," she said, so breathless she might as well have begged him to make good on his threat.

Lucas tried to do the gentlemanly thing, but despite

his efforts, his grin broke. He reached for her hand. "You want to stop?"

Staring at their intertwined fingers, she sighed. "We're too close. It doesn't make sense."

"Who cares about that?"

It still amazed her how much he seemed to want her all the time. Although he was careful around other people, he clearly had no problem being obvious with her. She wondered how he would behave toward her at the prison among people he knew.

Until this morning she'd had no idea they were going to the prison where he'd served his sentence. He'd told her after he'd picked her up. The shock hadn't completely worn off yet. "Will it be weird going back there?"

Traffic had increased, so he let go of her hand to hold on to the steering wheel. He waited until he'd changed lanes, then shook his head. "I've already been back twice. Once to visit a friend and then for PRN business."

"Well, the warden apparently likes you or he wouldn't be giving up part of his Saturday."

"We get along." He shrugged. "He's a decent guy. Strict but fair. And he supports the Wild Horse Training Program one hundred percent."

"Your friend… Is he still there?"

"He got out two months ago. Found a good job in Alaska, so that should help him keep his nose clean."

"Did he train horses?"

"Yep. Jimmy is the perfect success story. He walked into that prison one mean, ornery son of a bitch. You looked at him wrong and he'd stomp you into the ground. Even the guards hated tangling with him. Five years later he left a different man."

"I'm surprised they let him into the program." She saw Lucas's mouth tighten but she felt her point was valid. "I think it's great everything turned out well, but there was no way of knowing beforehand that he'd come through. I don't want to pick a fight here. I'm just trying to understand how the person you described was selected."

"Fair enough," Lucas said. "I vouched for him."

Well, that just raised a whole bunch of other questions. Now that she wasn't drowning in her own personal drama, she wondered if this trip had anything to do with him trying to prove something to her. Or did he even care what she thought? She'd be wise not to get ahead of herself. "No offense, but weren't you just another inmate?"

"I was involved with PRN by then, and I'd been working with Jimmy on his anger issues. Apparently I'd made more headway than the facility's shrink, though that's not saying much." His expression remained detached. "I'm not going to lie to you—my first year there, I was filled with rage. I refused to see my mom or stepfather or my sister, even after they'd traveled hours to see me. By then Peggy wasn't an issue. But there were days when I didn't even recognize myself."

"Peggy? Was she your girlfriend?"

"We were engaged. I'd asked her to marry me the week before I was arrested."

Surprised, Melanie stared at his profile. He seemed relaxed, his grip loose on the wheel. And since he'd brought up the subject, she saw no reason not to ask the obvious. "What happened? Did you get married and it didn't work out?"

"We called it off. Luckily, her folks were away on a cruise when I proposed. Peggy was real close to them and wanted to keep it a secret until they got back. The ring I gave her needed to be sized. The jeweler said it would take a week, and by then her parents would be home. We were going to tell them together." He shrugged. "I was arrested the day before they came back."

"So?"

A faint smile curved his mouth. "Getting slapped in handcuffs kind of trumped everything else." He glanced over at her. "The engagement wasn't a complete surprise. I'd bought the ranch the year before and was fixing it up so I'd have a home to offer her."

Melanie felt as if her insides had been twisted into a knot. "Did she ever tell them?"

"What was the point?" Lucas didn't seem angry or sad or anything. So why did this make her feel a little sick? "Peggy's best friend knew, but no one else."

"She just left you?"

"No, she stuck by me through the trial." He tugged at her hand. "Hey, Peggy's not a bad person. I told her not to wait for me. I encouraged her to move on. No one knew about the engagement, so it was easy to pretend it had never happened."

"Was it?" Even after such a short acquaintance, Melanie knew him better than that. Lucas wasn't the type to take marriage lightly. He'd poured his soul and sweat into a home for the woman he'd loved. And she'd abandoned him. "Was it easy?"

He sighed. "No."

"Do you still love her?"

"No," he said without hesitation. "She's married, has a son and is expecting a girl in a few months. She's happy, and I'm happy for her."

For a man who had no use for religion, he was a better person than Melanie. She harbored no such goodwill toward the woman who'd hurt him. Quite badly, Melanie guessed.

He squeezed her hand. "I'm glad you're here."

"Me too," she whispered. "Me too."

15

MELANIE OPENED THE motel-room door and Lucas brought their bags in behind her. He'd offered to get two rooms. She'd told him one would be fine, but she was nervous about the whole thing. Though it wasn't as if anyone from home knew where she was staying. Heck, *she* didn't even know where she was staying. The ten-unit building was a weird pinkish-gray color, set back from the highway, and it had an odd name. That was all she could remember.

Lucas closed the door and she jumped. He set the bags down on the floor and placed his hands on her shoulders. "You can have your own room. I won't be upset."

"You wouldn't?"

He shook his head. "No, I wouldn't. I want you to feel comfortable."

"Liar."

"Hey." He tried to look offended, but he couldn't fool her. "I didn't say I wouldn't be disappointed," he said, moving his hands down her arms and then pulling her against him. "Which bed do you want?"

She glanced at the pair of queen beds with the hideous pink bedspreads and laughed. "You choose first."

"Whichever one you're in."

"How did I know you were going to say that?" She tilted her head back, closing her eyes as he kissed her and then stopped too soon.

"You want to eat now or later?" he asked against her mouth.

In answer she yanked his shirt from his jeans.

The bags stayed right where they were on the floor by the door. Lucas unfastened her blouse buttons with impressive speed. His patience slipped when he went for the zipper of her jeans and their arms got tangled because she hadn't finished with his shirt. He took over, stripping off her clothes first and then his own.

She tried not to stare. Tried not to wonder how he'd gotten his jeans off without hurting himself. He was so hard already and they'd barely kissed. "You know what," she said. "I think I want a shower."

He was staring, too, first at her breasts and then into her eyes. "I was thinking the same thing." He slid his palm behind her neck. "Mind making room for me?"

"As long as you don't get any bigger."

Not moving, he just looked at her, and then he laughed.

Melanie let out a small whimper. "I didn't mean to say that out loud."

"Come here," he said, still laughing as he caught her before she could escape to the bathroom.

"I'm embarrassed," she admitted, slowly turning to him, and then he was holding her close and kissing her neck and lifting her into his strong muscled arms.

"Not with me, honey," he whispered. "Don't ever be embarrassed with me."

He'd managed to get them into the small bathroom and to turn on the shower before she knew what was happening. While he adjusted the water temperature, he kissed her lips and each of her breasts, and then she watched as he took her pearled nipple into his mouth. Kept watching as he suckled her, his stubbled jaw working greedily against her pale skin until her knees threatened to buckle.

She clutched his shoulders, and he lifted her into the stall.

"I should shave first," he said, frowning at the slight redness on her skin and rubbing the side of his jaw.

"No." She pulled him toward her. "Please."

"I don't want to hurt you."

"You won't." She held on so tight she gave him no choice.

He stepped into the stall, backing her up against the wall, pinning her bottom and shoulder blades against the cool tiles. She barely had time to let her head fall back before he caught her lip between his teeth, tugging gently, his breathing coming faster and more urgently. Huffs of warm breath slipped into her mouth along with his tongue.

Her own eagerness had her shaking, her whole body throbbing with a craving that both frightened and excited her. No other man had ever lit this fire inside her, awakened this intense ache between her legs. Lucas knew exactly what she needed. He plunged deeper into her mouth, thrusting his tongue against hers and swallowing her quiet whimpers. He cupped both of her breasts, kneading them with unsteady hands. She could feel his erection, the thick hot flesh, straining against her belly. At some point her hands had closed into fists, and she slowly opened her fingers and touched his chest, ran her thumb across a hard beaded nipple. She skimmed her other palm lower until the heel brushed the silken head of his penis. For a moment he stilled, and so did she.

He tore his mouth away from hers, drew in some air, expelled a harsh breath. "Do it, Melanie," he said, his voice husky and raw. "Touch me."

She leaned into him, burying her face against his shoulder as she closed her hand around his fully aroused cock.

He shuddered, and she licked his arm, traced her tongue over a ridge of muscle, tasting the saltiness of his skin. She tightened her hold and felt him jerk against her palm as she stroked upward.

Releasing her breasts, he pulled away, dislodging her hand. Blindly he reached behind, slapping the tiles until he found the soap. It was still wrapped, and he let out a short growl of impatience while trying to tear off the paper.

"You have to stop doing this to me," she said, frustration making her bold. The man was gorgeous. Absolutely beautiful. And all hers—at least for now. And she wanted to touch him. She looked up when he didn't respond.

He wasn't listening. His gaze was fastened on her mouth. The soap was in his hand, the wrapper gone. "What?" he murmured.

"Not letting me touch you."

Lucas met her eyes. "Right now I want you too much."

"Last time you said, 'Later.'" She splayed her fingers across his chest, slid her hand to his waist. "This is later."

A faint smile lifted the corner of his mouth. "You can't starve a man, dangle a banquet in front of him and expect him to take only one bite."

"Same goes for a woman."

The smile reached his eyes. He bent to steal a kiss, but before she could get him in her grasp, he lowered himself and kissed each breast. Then pressed his damp mouth to a spot between her ribs while he slid his soapy hands around to her back.

Until now his body had shielded her from the shower spray. But with him crouching, water bounced off his shoulders and splashed her face. Startled and laughing, she abandoned her mission and tried to twist away. His large hands cupped her bottom, holding her still as he put his mouth on the damp heat between her thighs.

She stiffened, wouldn't let his seeking lips in too far,

even as she held his head prisoner. She jerked at the feel of his tongue, hot and determined, the rough tip pushing past the sensitive folds of flesh, teasing her, tempting her to part for him.

"Lucas," she murmured, her voice a breathy thread of a whisper.

"Let me taste you." The slight vibration of his lips nearly drove her to the edge. "Please, Melanie." He sounded as if he'd run a marathon. "Please."

She relaxed and let him spread her thighs a little, wedging his hand between them. Touching her first with his thumb, parting her, stroking her, before pushing his tongue against her and taking long broad licks that sent her up on her toes.

He squeezed her butt, and she bucked against his mouth.

His groan sounded like a curse. It might've been one. Her senses had gone haywire. All she knew for sure was that her response had triggered him in a big way. He'd tried to slow down, then got carried away, sucking and licking and thrusting his tongue until she nearly lost her mind. She wanted to get out of the shower. Get to the bed while she could still walk. Still breathe.

"Lucas, let's get out. Let's— Oh." She gasped at the first jolt. "Oh…oh, God."

It was too late to do anything but hold on to him.

The spasms rolled through her, setting off bursts of pleasure that swelled up from between her thighs to her breasts. She bit down hard on her lip, trying to stifle the cry rising from her throat. Tears burned behind her eyes, and he kept flicking his tongue, ignoring her panic and setting off a firestorm of blazing sensations that threatened to incinerate her.

His strong fingers, digging into her buttocks, were the only thing holding her up as she rode out the inferno. Weak and shaky, she fell back, her head hitting the tile a bit hard, but she didn't care. Her energy had been sapped, and it was enough that she hadn't slid down to the shower floor.

Lucas must've realized that he'd wrung everything out of her. His lips took over for his tongue and he brushed soft featherlike kisses up her belly to her breasts as he rose. The gentle controlled meeting of their mouths surprised her. Not on her part—she still had trouble staying on her feet. But Lucas's body was tense, his arousal even harder than before.

He lifted his mouth off hers, and she looked into eyes so dark there was no trace of blue. "We're going to make this fast," he murmured, his voice husky and deep.

She didn't know what he meant until she felt the soap glide between her breasts up to her throat. No lingering this time. In seconds he'd lathered her entire body, and then it was her turn. She started with his back and butt, feeling the tension humming through him. Skipping his legs for now, she guided the soap to his chest. She looked down at the broad head of his penis and her lips parted on a gasp.

The soap flew out of her hand as he lifted her in his arms and placed her under the shower spray. He took a half-turn, got some of the suds off himself, then shut off the water.

Melanie laughed. "We're not finished."

"No, we're not," he said and grabbed a pair of white towels off the rack. His rough kiss made it clear what he was talking about, and already she was starting to ache for him in places that should've been sated.

The towels were pretty awful, slightly scratchy, or maybe it was her skin's sensitivity. Lucas dried both of them, leaving too many damp areas in his rush to get them to the bed. He had trouble pulling back the quilt, and she laughed when he finally wrestled it to the floor.

Her humor met with an abrupt end when she saw what he pulled out of his bag. "You brought a whole box?"

He set the condoms on the nightstand between the beds. "You have a problem with that?"

"No." The word came out a squeak. "No," she repeated with more conviction, her gaze inexorably going to his cock.

She slipped under the covers on her side, instantly realizing there were no sides with Lucas. He yanked the sheet and thin blanket to the foot of the bed and slid his naked body up hers. His skin was damp and hot, his mouth even hotter as he nipped at her breast, lightly tugging at her nipple with his teeth. When she squirmed he moved to her lips, kissed her briefly, then fastened on to her earlobe while slipping a hand between her thighs.

"You ready for me?" he murmured against her ear and sank a finger deep inside her. They moaned together. "Jesus."

He withdrew his finger, drawing moisture out with it and spreading it around her opening until she thought she'd hit the ceiling.

Quickly he tore open a packet, then sheathed himself and moved between her legs. One arm supported his weight while he guided himself inside her. He took the first push slow and easy, his attempt at restraint clear.

Melanie didn't want him to hold back. All it took to let him know was a small lift of her hips.

Lucas bit off a curse, looked into her eyes and pushed hard into her. The whole mattress moved. She clutched the sheets so tightly she thought they might rip.

"Harder," she whispered.

He stayed where he was, braced on one elbow, looking down at her. And then he was moving inside her, never looking away, muscles cording along his neck and across his shoulders.

The pressure was building in her again, and she kind of wished he'd just lose control. He was so ready. How could he hold back? "You still want it hard?" His breathing had grown so harsh he barely got the words out.

She nodded and he drew back, then drove into her. Spurred on by her startled whimper, he kept rocking his hips, each thrust forcing him deeper inside her body. She tensed, her muscles gripping his erection and tearing a groan from him.

In seconds his taut body went still, and then he shuddered violently. Even before he finished climaxing he tried to reach between them, tried to find the sensitive nub that would make her crazy, but she shoved his hand away, wanting only to hold him in her arms through the last of the shock waves, just as he'd held her.

Too weak to argue, he sagged heavily against her until the tremors subsided. "Well, Teach." He kissed her, then rolled onto his back. "We've got some serious homework to do."

"Really?" She let him slide his arm under her shoulders and draw her close so she could snuggle against him. "What's that?"

"We have to work on our timing." He turned on his side, bringing his other arm around her so they lay face-to-face.

"Timing?"

His eyes were serious, his nod somber. "Don't get me wrong.... I like giving you an orgasm right off the bat. But after that I'd like it if we could practice coming at the same time."

Startled, Melanie just stared at him. Then let out a laugh.

"Hey, I'm serious."

"I see that." She ordered herself not to blush, then did anyway. "I must admit, I wasn't prepared for this conversation."

Lucas flashed a shameless smile.

"You're enjoying my embarrassment? Really?" She got him back by pretending she was getting out of bed.

"Honey, no." He tightened his arms around her, struggling to look contrite and failing miserably. "I'm not trying to embarrass you." He kissed her nose, then her lips and started rubbing her back, his hand moving in a slow caress. "I'm serious...." He found the spot by her ear that drove her wild. "I want to be inside you when you come."

"How serious?"

"Very." He traced her bottom lip with his tongue. "Extremely serious."

"All that homework," she murmured, getting into the swing of things. "It's a pity we have only two days."

His hand stopped moving. He stared into her face, his eyes narrowing...enough for her to wonder if she'd said something wrong.

"Lucas?"

He blinked, his mouth relaxing into a smile, and she nearly sighed with relief. "You're right, honey," he said, continuing the rhythmic stroking along her spine. "We don't have much time, so we'd better get to it."

"I don't even care if we skip dinner."

"You might later."

No, she wouldn't, but she felt no need to correct him. She did need a kiss, though, and pressed one to his lips. He accepted it as an invitation to slide a hand down to her butt and pull her against him. He was half-hard already.

"Wait," she said. "I want to ask you something before I forget."

"What?" His impatient frown thrilled her all the way down to her toes.

"Isn't your ranch near here?"

"About an hour." A wary expression settled on his face. "Why?"

"Show it to me."

Lucas released her and exhaled a harsh sigh. "It's in bad shape, Melanie," he said, shaking his head. "I can't take you over there."

"I know you travel a lot for PRN. I didn't expect you'd have it back in tip-top condition yet," she said and felt the tension ripple through him. What on earth was wrong with her? She was being horribly insensitive. The place had to remind him of Peggy and their broken engagement. "Never mind." She smiled. "It was just a thought."

He focused on the ceiling. "I've only been back once."

"Since you were released?" she asked, and when he nodded, she felt a lump forming in her throat. He might want to believe he was over his ex-fiancée, but clearly he wasn't. "I'm sorry I brought it up."

"The bastard still lives there."

"Who?"

"Cal Jessup. His ranch still borders mine and I know I shouldn't let—" Lucas stopped and frowned at her as if she'd just gone off the deep end.

Realizing her silly smile was inappropriate, she sobered. "That's horrible. Of course you wouldn't want to run into him." Seeing that he was still confused, she let out a sigh. "I thought it was about Peggy. That you still had feelings for her. Not that it's any of my business."

It was Lucas's turn to smile. He shifted back to his old position, hugged her against his chest. "No, Peggy has nothing to do with it. She has what she wants," he said and kissed Melanie's hair. "And I have what *I* want."

The huskiness in his voice sent a jolt of pure joy through her. She knew he didn't mean her, but for a few hours what was the harm in pretending? He tightened his hold, and contentment settled over her like a warm fleece blanket. Nothing mattered more than the safety and comfort of his arms around her, feeling the slow steady beat of his heart against her breast and knowing he wanted her.

For now, nothing mattered more than being with Lucas.

16

HE WOKE FROM the best dream, only to find it really was Melanie's hand brushing over his cock, her lips meandering across his chest. He growled low in his throat, stopping her dead still. For a second.

Her chuckle sounded pretty smug as she went right on with her exploration. The feel of her body pressing against him was as much of a turn-on as her featherlight touch. Damn if he wasn't getting addicted to her silky skin.

The only problem with this was his need to touch her. To pull her in tight and slide between those amazing thighs. He groaned as he lifted his head. Moved his hand to her nape.

Her lips, still ghosting over his flesh, curled up just before they swept over his nipple. The tip of her tongue made him jerk, and he pressed too hard on the back of her neck.

She returned the favor with a squeeze that was just enough to make him moan and ache for more.

"Come up here," he said, his voice hoarse.

"Why? I'm having a good time."

"Hey, and I'm loving it. But we still haven't perfected—"

"Our synchronized coming?" she said, lifting her head up enough to meet his gaze.

He couldn't stand it another second. With her tousled hair and wicked grin, she was everything he'd imagined during those long years alone. No, way better than his paltry imagination had managed. It didn't take much to help her up, and the soft purring sound she made when they kissed lit up something deep inside.

She gasped when he spun her over so she was beneath him. No more teasing. He needed her too much, and from the wild look in her eyes, she was on the same page.

"I want—"

"Take it," she whispered.

He nabbed a condom and somehow lived through the long seconds it took to put it on. The whole time, he looked into her eyes, drowning and not caring. The pull to be around her, in her, was a force he barely understood.

As he thrust into her wet heat, he took her mouth in a bruising kiss, and despite the danger of hoping for too much, all he could think was *Mine.*

SOMEHOW, THEY MADE IT to the prison and past the first security point on time. They signed in and presented their IDs. Even Lucas had turned over his driver's license since it was a matter of protocol for any visitor. He knew all but one guard, who was new. Employees here at Wilcox tended to be lifers. Good thing he'd gotten along well with most of them. They hadn't been surprised to see him. Obviously, word had spread that Lucas was the reason the warden was coming in on his day off.

He lightly touched Melanie's lower back, steering her toward the hall that led to the warden's office. "You nervous?"

"No." She turned to him. "Should I be?"

The door clanged shut behind them, and she jumped.

He managed a smile, but he'd about leaped out of his skin himself. The sound vividly reminded him of lockdown. You never knew how or when the confinement ended. Whether you'd be stuck for hours or days without seeing the sun or getting any fresh air because some hothead had threatened a guard.

As the hall veered right, he lowered his hand. They'd talked about keeping a professional front. No one needed to know how he felt about her. Hell, *he* wasn't even sure how he felt about her. He had a damn good inkling. He just didn't know what he should do about it.

The institutional smell still got to him. But then, he could be two hundred miles away and swear the stink of disinfectant and desperation still clung to the air. He wondered if that would ever go away.

He spotted a familiar figure coming toward them and grinned. "Hey, Charlie, how's the arm?"

The older guard had been too busy eyeing Melanie to notice Lucas. At the sound of his voice, Charlie scowled and rolled his shoulder. "It does just fine until some knucklehead reminds me I should've had that surgery by now." He stopped in front of them and offered a toothy grin to Melanie.

She smiled back, and man, if that didn't put a twinkle in the old guy's eye.

He extended a hand to Lucas. "Good to see you, son. Usually I'm off today. I would've hated to miss you."

"I figured you'd retired by now."

Charlie snorted. "That ain't gonna work out. I mention the *R* word and the missus starts making lists of everything that needs fixing." He rubbed a hand over his bald pate. "Nooo, if I'm gonna bust my rump, I might as well get paid for it."

"Smart man." Lucas clapped him on his good shoulder. "Well, we gotta go. We're here to see Jack."

"Yeah, he's back there. If you've got time before you leave, find me. Nice meeting you, ma'am."

Lucas got them moving again, then said to Melanie, who was watching him with a puzzled expression, "I didn't introduce you on purpose. I start doing that with every guy who wants to shoot the breeze and we'd be here all day."

She resumed walking alongside him. "Jack?" she said. "As in Warden Fowler?"

"Yep. Sometimes I call him Warden, sometimes Jack. Especially when I'm talking to someone like Charlie. He and the warden go way back. Why? Does it bother you?"

"No, of course not, but I am surprised."

Another guard passed them. Lucas greeted him by name, and Roger mentioned how everyone still missed seeing him in the library.

Melanie glanced over her shoulder. "These men are all guards, right?" She waited for him to nod. "This is crazy. They're treating you like you're a former frat brother."

They'd just reached the deserted reception area. The warden's office sat in the back, and before Lucas could respond, the door opened. Dressed casually in jeans and a brown knit shirt, Jack walked toward them.

"I thought I heard your voice. Always good to see you, Sloan," he said. He shook hands with both of them and introduced himself to Melanie. He wasn't much of a talker, friendly but to the point. "You mind heading over to the farm right away?"

"Let's go," Lucas said, anxious to be outdoors. He honestly hadn't thought coming back would bother him, though he suspected his unease had more to do with what Melanie might be thinking.

"I hate rushing you folks but I promised my grandsons a day of fishing." For a short guy, the warden moved fast.

"Hey, we appreciate you taking the time," Lucas said. "I'll be honest with you, Warden. Melanie doesn't need convincing. It's some of her board members who aren't sure."

"There always has to be someone in the bunch." Jack smiled at Melanie as he held open a door for them. "So it's your job to report back and win them over."

She nodded. "I'm going to do my best."

"I've had my secretary compile statistics on the lower recidivism rates, an accounting of the money the program brings in and an explanation as to how candidates are chosen to do the training. Hopefully, that'll give you some help."

Lucas followed Melanie outside and deeply inhaled the crisp morning air. He'd always preferred the outdoors, but after being cooped up for three years, not much compared to blue sky and a mountain breeze.

Jack was watching him, a small knowing smile deepening the grooves in his weathered cheeks. The warden didn't miss much—good thing, given the nature of his job. Unfortunately, he'd also noticed the protective hand Lucas had absently pressed to Melanie's back.

Pretending their relationship was strictly professional was a smart idea. But he knew he'd screw up. After this morning, he desperately wanted to touch her, whether it was her arm, her face, her hair....

"Oh." Her eyes widened with delight at the handsome black stallion being led out of the stable for his training.

"That young fella is going to fetch a nice price at next month's auction." Jack squinted against the sun's glare. "So is the chestnut gelding coming out behind him."

"They're beautiful. Both of them." She reached for Lucas's hand and entwined it with hers.

He just smiled and squeezed.

BY THE TIME Melanie realized what she'd done, it was too late. The warden and the men leading the horses had seen her grab Lucas's hand. She promptly let go and muttered, "Sorry."

"It's okay," he whispered. "I'm sure they would've figured it out anyway."

The warden graciously ignored her faux pas and went on to explain what to expect on the tour. She tried to concentrate on what he was saying, but she was distracted by Lucas's comment. Why would anyone think they were involved?

"...with the corrals and equipment sheds in the back but I'm guessing you're more interested in the training," the warden was saying, and she forced herself to pay attention.

The stable looked freshly painted, and the barn roof was definitely new. All the buildings seemed to be in terrific condition. Better than Safe Haven, even with its recent infusion of cash. There was more lawn than gravel, something she envied, the grass neatly mowed and trimmed and still very green for late September.

Warden Fowler explained that they had several areas for training, both outside and indoors, and led them toward a large building that looked like a warehouse. Near the double doors, two men wearing faded chambray shirts were unloading boxes from a trailer. They stopped to stare at Melanie.

She managed to give them a smile and felt horrible for feeling so nervous. Yes, they were obviously inmates, but she had nothing to fear from them.

"All right, fellas, keep working," the warden said drily. "We know you've seen a woman before."

"Not one this pretty." The taller burly man gave her a crooked grin and pulled off his beanie.

Melanie blushed, and Lucas slid his arm around her.

Glancing at Lucas, the man's face lit with surprise. "Hey, Sloan. I didn't even see you."

"Yeah, I noticed," Lucas said with wry, faint humor. "She's taken. Find your own woman, Dawson."

The warden and the other inmate laughed.

"That was low," Dawson said in a gruff voice, though there was no hostility in his face. "I didn't expect that from you."

"Sorry, buddy, I wasn't thinking." Grinning, Lucas lowered his arm from her shoulders. "You're outta here soon, right?"

Dawson pressed his palms together as if in prayer, briefly glancing skyward. "The good Lord willin'." He cast an exaggerated look of fondness at the warden. "And with my friend Warden Fowler's recommendation."

"So why haven't you gotten back to work?" the warden asked, his stern expression not fooling anyone.

"Yes, sir." Dawson stuck the beanie back on his head. "We got some real good tack this time if you wanna have a look-see later."

"Monday," Jack said, already moving on. "I'm going fishing."

"See ya, Sloan." Dawson stooped to heft a box. "Hopefully on the outside."

"Call when you get out. You have my number." Lucas was touching her lower back again and guiding her toward the double doors.

"'Bye, pretty lady."

Melanie laughed and lifted her hand in a small wave. Lucas was smiling at her. "What?"

"Nothing." Nothing her foot. She knew that amused look of his, but she could hardly make an issue of it in front of the warden.

"Those boxes the men were unloading are donations," Jack said once they were inside. "The ranchers around here are good about sending over used jeans, boots and tack that's still in decent condition."

"Nice that you have their support." She glanced around, amazed at the huge arena, the rows of ascending bleachers on three sides.

"Primarily the training is done outside. During inclement weather or if there's a difficult stallion, we use this area." The warden gestured to a man working with a paint. "We hold the auctions here, as well. On any given adoption day, it's not unusual to have over a hundred people packed in here. Some are looking to bid, but a lot of them just come to watch. They like seeing what the prisoners have accomplished." He paused, watching the trainer and horse with pride. "We're small potatoes compared to some of the other prison farms, but we do all right."

"Well, damn," Lucas muttered, and she turned and followed his gaze to another man on the opposite side of the arena running a currycomb over a roan colt. "Good for Diego. He finally got admitted into the program. Is this his first horse?"

"Second, I believe." They watched in silence for a few moments. "Too bad Bob isn't here—Baker's in charge of this particular program," the warden added for Melanie's benefit. "He knows the details better than I do. Naturally, I had to force him to take vacation this week," he said wryly, then glanced at Lucas. "You probably know more than I do."

He shrugged. "Look, Jack, you gave us the official meet and greet, which we appreciate. Melanie knows enough about how the program works. If you don't mind us poking around by ourselves, you should take off. Make Charlie babysit us if you don't feel comfortable giving me free—"

The warden snorted a laugh as if the notion was absurd. He glanced at his watch. "You know how strongly I feel about the program." He looked at Melanie. "I'd hate to duck out early if I can help with something that might convince your people."

"I love seeing the program in action, and hopefully, my enthusiasm will carry over when I report to the board. But I agree with Lucas. Don't keep your grandsons waiting."

Jack smiled. "Tell you what—you folks take your time and I'll leave that paperwork in the reception area. And if you still have board members straddling the fence, feel free to have them call me. I'll do what I can to put any fears to rest."

"Thank you," Melanie said, knowing there was no way she could allow anyone other than Shea to speak with the warden. Ridiculous. A grown woman worrying about people knowing she had a boyfriend. Though she really didn't know what she and Lucas were to each other.

Right before the warden left, she overheard him quietly tell Lucas that if he had time, someone named Watson could use his advice because his public defender was an idiot. Lucas nodded and agreed to call as they shook hands.

Once they were on their own, they sat on the bleachers and watched the horses and trainers go through their paces. Lucas told her what he knew of the prisoners, how they'd change as time went by, and she was very impressed with how much pride was in each one of them.

And Lucas… He was amazing in so many ways a woman would have to be crazy or stupid not to want him. She was neither, and with sudden clarity she knew she had some changes to make. There was something fundamentally wrong in hiding her feelings for a good man like Lucas. It was time her parents and everyone else realized she was a normal, red-blooded woman entitled to her own life.

They took the same route back to the office to pick up the paperwork the warden had left for them. The statistics were going to be helpful, especially for the board members who were on the fence. There wasn't much new, aside from the setup, that she'd learned from the warden, but coming here had been tremendously valuable all the same. She'd never have gotten the feel of what the program accomplished in any other way.

It was almost two o'clock when they finally climbed

into the truck. Melanie was exhausted from too little sleep and information overload, but that didn't stop her mind from racing with questions. None of which pertained to the Wild Horse Training Program.

As soon as they'd arrived, she'd realized that she'd subconsciously been stewing, fretting that seeing him in the prison environment would be depressing. She'd never expected the opposite to be true.

"Hey, pretty lady."

She turned to him with a laugh.

"How's my girl?" he asked, leaning over the console, his blue eyes full of sexy mischief.

She reared back a breath away from his kiss. "Your *girl?*"

"That's what everyone in there thinks."

Her heart thudded. "And you?"

"Me?" He slid a hand behind her neck. "I think I might kidnap you," he murmured and brushed his warm lips across hers.

"Keep that up and I might let you," she whispered, her voice garbled against his mouth. More and more it seemed she had no willpower when it came to Lucas. No common sense. No self-preservation. The situation was becoming quite desperate, she thought vaguely when she heard a nearby car door slam and blithely ignored it.

He startled her by breaking the kiss. His hand moved from her neck to cup the side of her face. "I've changed my mind," he said, searching her eyes. "I want to show you my ranch."

LUCAS KNEW WHAT he would find, and yet seeing the barn door sagging from its hinges, half the corral posts lying in the dirt and the grain shed leaning to the left still got to him. Aware that Melanie was watching him, he parked the truck in front of the modest brick house with the long porch he'd built himself. Peggy had always wanted a wraparound porch, but he'd run out of wood and money and figured he'd extend it later, after they were married.

"We can go inside," he said, opening his door. "But I'll warn you, there isn't much furniture, and the kitchen isn't equipped. A few basic cooking utensils, but that's it."

"And here I thought you were going to whip me up a gourmet lunch." She rolled her eyes and climbed out. "Oh, what a cool weather vane," she said, staring up at the barn roof.

He smiled. The place was falling down around them and she noticed the copper horse. "I want to have a look at the porch steps before we go inside, make sure nothing's rotted. They should've had another coat of seal before… life got interrupted."

She came around the hood of the truck, put her arms around his waist and studied the front of the house. "Cute place. I love the green shutters. Did you do that?"

Nodding, he pushed his fingers through her hair, liking how the sun brought out wisps of honey-colored highlights.

Her eyes drifted closed for a moment. Then she tilted her head back to look at him. "If this gets too hard for you, we leave, okay?"

"When I first got out, coming here was tough. I knew the livestock had been turned over to Jessup as restitution, and man, did that piss me off." He surveyed the barn, which had doubled as a stable until he could build one. "But I'm fine. These are just things. They can be repaired or replaced."

She sighed. "It'll take quite a bit of money, but then, you don't have to rush, either."

"Money isn't a problem. It's not as if I'm loaded but I have a small inheritance from my grandmother. Enough to fix up the place and buy more livestock…if that's what I decide to do."

"Your grandmother died while you were in prison?" she asked, her eyes wide.

"She'd already been suffering from dementia by the time I went to trial. Kind of a mixed blessing since she had no idea what was going on. I still wish I could've gone to her funeral." He saw the moist sympathy in Melanie's eyes and let her go so he could check the steps. No use getting emotional along with her.

"I'm so sorry, Lucas."

"Yeah, me too." Crouching, he tested the wood's condition. "It's going to be warm inside. The windows are locked tight to keep out critters."

"I don't care if it's a hundred in there. I'm excited to see it." She offered him a hand up, then leaned in for a kiss.

He readily obliged, tasting her soft eager mouth and wanting to lift her into his arms and make love to her right here on the porch. "I should warn you," he said, before he got carried away. "I'm seriously considering the kidnapping thing. I like how you are away from Blackfoot Falls."

Melanie grinned. "It is nice to be myself," she said, rubbing up against him.

His cock had already taken an interest and her little bump and grind wasn't helping. "This is going to be a very short tour and then we're finding a motel."

"Deal." She laughed when he had to finally pick her up and firmly set her away from him. "Hey, I've never been with a celebrity before."

"Huh?"

"At the prison, everyone wanted to see you."

"Not everyone," he said, unlocking the front door and thinking about Batshit-Crazy Bubba, who'd occupied the cell next to him.

"The guys training horses all wanted to show off for you. They were tickled pink that you were proud of them."

He entered the house first to make sure there were no

nasty surprises. The couch, cherry side table and plaid recliner were still there. That didn't mean they hadn't been infested with vermin. Her teasing finally stirred his memory. "Honey, I'm sorry but I've got to make a quick call to the prison. I want to do it while Charlie is still on shift so he'll patch me through. You mind wandering around on your own for a few minutes?"

"Right. You have to call Mr. Watson," she said, as she trailed her fingers across the back of the couch. "Another fan, I presume."

"Better watch out for mice."

She jumped and snatched back her hand. "Why would the warden ask you to advise a prisoner?"

Lucas sighed. "Don't repeat that. Jack shouldn't be getting involved."

"No, of course not. You don't have to tell me."

He shrugged. "When I wasn't training horses, I spent a lot of time in the library. I liked reading law books. I picked up pointers and passed them on. That's all."

Melanie smiled. She looked so relaxed and happy. As she had that night after dinner at the Sundance and when they'd been alone, sneaking kisses at Safe Haven. When she was around town or with other people, she always seemed tense, on guard.

All because of him. Because of this crazy thing they had between them. It was happening so fast it was like being swept up in a whirlwind. If he was this blown away by how much he cared for her in so short a time, what must it be like for Melanie, living her whole life under a microscope and needing to watch what she said and did… how she reacted to him? Their relationship had put her in a difficult position.

It bothered him that she was more comfortable away from home. He wondered if she even realized it should be the other way around. Home was supposed to be the place where she should feel free to be herself.

He wondered if Blackfoot Falls had become Melanie's prison.

17

MONDAY DRAGGED BY so slowly it was painful. Melanie had a headache that had started at school earlier, and now seeing Lucas at Safe Haven didn't help.

She stood behind Susie and Ben, supervising the grain distribution, carefully keeping her back to Lucas as he worked on the corral. She hadn't realized it would be this hard. It hurt not being able to touch him when she wanted or react to his smile. In a way, spending the weekend with him had been a mistake.

Realistically, the emptiness inside her had probably seeded long before she'd met Lucas. But at least before, the ache had been bearable. Last night after he'd dropped her off, she was so exhausted she should've been asleep instantly, and not staring into the darkness playing guessing games with herself.

Lucas already had a full life, and on the ride back he'd confided that he was seriously considering getting his ranch in shape. His work with PRN was still a priority for him. And it turned out Ernie Watson wasn't the only prisoner who was counting on Lucas to help him navigate the legal system.

That left very little time for her. Assuming he even

wanted to maintain their relationship. He'd hinted he did, but she wasn't good at picking up those kinds of cues. She knew with absolute certainty that Lucas hadn't used her, that he cared for her. But that didn't mean he wanted more. Making love didn't mean that he loved her. And what had she gone and done?

Hugging herself, she rocked back on the heels of her work boots. Tonight the board would meet again. She'd give them her report and they would vote. No telling how that would go. If they turned down PRN, there'd be no reason for Lucas to stick around.

"Jeez, Mel." Shea's voice pulled her out of her misery. "I didn't know you two got home so late yesterday. I should've asked the board to meet tomorrow. We can call everyone and change it."

"We didn't return *that* late," she muttered. "Although to hear my father tell it, you'd think I'd practically eloped."

Shea smiled. "See, that's why I don't live near either of my parents." She leaned closer. "Did you have fun?"

Melanie couldn't help but smile. "Um, wow."

"I knew it." Shea seemed pleased. "He keeps watching you. So don't look."

"We're not in high school," Melanie said but couldn't stifle her grin.

Her students turned to stare at her, their noses wrinkled.

She cleared her throat. "Okay, guys, we're going to leave ten minutes early. Help me round up everyone, okay?" She waited for them to exit the barn. "Shea, do me a favor and tell Lucas I think it's better we go to the meeting separately." She took a few steps. "And if he wants, we can grab a bite to eat afterward."

Shea frowned. "Why don't you just call him?"

Startled, Melanie opened her mouth, but what could she say? She was being ridiculous. She was free to go talk to him right now if she wanted. What was it that made her feel this silly need to be…a saint? The thought struck quite a blow. She'd been so confident at the prison. So sure she could face her father and everyone else on her own terms.

Shea patted Melanie's arm. "It's all right, Mel. I'll tell him. You worry about getting the kids back to school."

Heaven help her—if she made it through the day without falling apart, it would be a miracle.

SHEA GAVE HER the floor and Melanie stood. Carefully avoiding Lucas on her right, she gazed out at the crowd, which had doubled since the last meeting. One thing Blackfoot Falls loved was a scandal.

Her father had come tonight, whether as Pastor Ray or a concerned dad, she wasn't sure. The moment she'd spotted him entering town hall, she'd known he'd head for the empty seat next to David. They sat in the front row with matching blank expressions, and she ordered herself to stay calm. So far she'd managed to avoid eye contact. But they were only three minutes into the meeting.

"Good evening, everyone." She stopped to clear her throat.

"I'm glad to see so many of you taking an interest in Safe Haven. We're always happy to have more volunteers, if you'd care to leave your name with Shea or myself."

Quiet murmurs and a few sour looks made her take a deep breath. "The Wild Horse Training Program works. As most of you know, I've been in favor of Safe Haven's participation from the beginning. To me it's always sounded like a win-win. And now that I've seen the program in action, I couldn't be more enthusiastic. The horses live in well-maintained stables, have excellent health care and thrive under the 'least resistance' training that's employed. Meaning the techniques used are rooted in equine behavior and positive reinforcement."

She made a point of addressing the other board members often, hoping to remind them that this would be their decision. And not the people sitting in the audience.

"Obviously, Warden Fowler, who runs the prison, endorses the program and is pleased with its therapeutic effects on the inmates. He's given me some statistics that I'd like to share with you." Dismayed to be fumbling with the material that she'd carefully arranged, she paused to take a sip of water. "Current research shows that just fifteen percent of the two hundred fifty men who've participated so far have returned to prison after being released, as compared to a twenty-five-percent recidivism rate for the rest of the state's prisons."

"That ain't so good," an audience member called out. "Fifteen percent got out and committed more crimes?"

The crowd started to murmur, and Melanie put up a hand, requesting silence.

"He also pointed out that the national average hovers somewhere around sixty percent. If you take that into consideration, fifteen percent is quite remarkable." Melanie glanced over to check Abe's and Cy's reactions. It didn't appear she'd won them over yet. "I probably should've stated earlier, Wilcox is a minimum-security facility, and so are all the prison farms that host the program, I believe," she said, looking at Lucas, who gave a small nod.

She hadn't needed confirmation. She'd known that, but she was getting more nervous. The few hotheads speaking out of turn weren't responsible. She'd expected some of that—she and Shea had agreed to let them speak as long as they weren't disruptive. It was her father sitting in the first row who was upsetting her, even as she refused to meet his eyes. She knew he was here, and she knew it was because of Lucas.

"They're still criminals," Earl griped from the back of the room. "We should worry about shipping in entertainment for them? Whatever happened to letting them rot?"

Melanie glared at the man. "What happened to our Christian duty to forgive and not judge?" She immediately regretted the words. And not just because some people were staring at her as if she'd gone over to the dark side. One thing she'd learned early—church members hated being reminded of their hypocrisy.

No, her regret stemmed from not keeping her own beliefs compartmentalized. This was about doing the right thing, but it wasn't a religious discussion. She swept an apologetic glance at the board and saw she hadn't gained any new allies.

Still refusing to look at her father or David, she briefly looked out at the audience and said, "I apologize for that remark." She cleared her throat and stared down at the piece of paper in front of her. "Let me explain how candidates for the program are selected."

She simply read from the paper, not trusting herself to ad-lib. She'd already blown it. Her rash words weren't to blame, though they hadn't helped. The moment she'd gone against conventional expectation and left Blackfoot Falls with Lucas, she'd condemned the program. And now they were going to take it out on him and PRN. She'd put her own needs first, and this was the result. How had she not foreseen this? Neither her father nor David had tripped her up. She'd done it all by herself.

More people started asking questions, and she was vaguely aware that one of them was David, but she could barely listen. She looked at Shea, who seemed to be waiting for a cue. "Can we end the meeting?" Melanie asked, panic rising in her throat. "Postpone the vote until everyone has had time to think?"

Ignoring shouted objections, Shea jumped to her feet.

Melanie sank back into her metal chair, resisting the overwhelming urge to flee. Silence descended for a moment, letting her take a breath. Shea would call an end to the meeting, and she'd be able to leave. But instead of Shea, Lucas said, "I have something I want to share with you folks."

He was on his feet and Shea was sitting again. Melanie swallowed and sat up straighter, trying to make sense of what was happening.

"I've known a number of prisoners who've gone through this program, and I've seen firsthand what a difference it's made in their lives. Men go to prison for all kinds of reasons. Some are hardened criminals who shouldn't be let out on the streets ever again."

"That's all of 'em," Earl shouted.

"And some have made mistakes," Lucas said, ignoring the taunt, "but they're not broken. Given the opportunity, they can come around, leave the system better men. That's what this program does. It reminds those who qualify that there's a life on the outside that's worth living. That's worth changing for."

"This is all just pop-psychology bull," Earl said, standing now. Looking as though he'd just been waiting for a fight. "You do-gooders don't have any real experience. All you got is textbooks and statistics."

Melanie stood up, held her hand out to put an end to Earl's tirade. Shea was right next to her, calling for order, but now the whole room was buzzing and nothing good could come from this. If she hadn't been so weak…

"Let me finish," Lucas said. "Please."

"We don't need to mollycoddle that kind of filth." Earl waved his hand around. "Giving 'em all ponies to play with."

"It's not like that," Lucas said, taking a step forward.

Melanie wanted to reach out to him, hold him back. She could see he was losing it, that it wasn't just Earl now; it was a bunch of folks standing up, everyone talking at once.

Shea and Jesse were trying to calm things down, but no one was listening.

"You're wrong," Lucas said, his voice rising above the fray. "Can't you see they aren't all animals? Those men deserve to have a second chance."

"What the hell do you know?" Earl shouted.

"Because I was one of them. This program saved my life."

Melanie gasped.

No. No. No.

The room got so quiet she could hear the blood rush in her ears. Lucas looked stricken. He didn't turn to face her but she could see he realized what he'd done, that he'd just confessed in front of her father, her boss and half the town.

And she slid headfirst from panic to complete and utter shock.

WHAT THE HELL had he done? Lucas wanted to take back his words, turn back time. But he couldn't. It didn't matter now what the vote was, what anyone thought of him. He'd just betrayed the woman he loved.

"I do hope you'll all give serious consideration to supporting PRN." His voice sounded as wrecked as he felt. "It'll help reduce Safe Haven's load, you won't ever have to worry about the horses, and in the end there'll be less crime."

He closed his eyes for a second just to gather the strength to face Melanie. When he did, she looked devastated. Her face was pale and her eyes were so wounded he wanted to drop to his knees and beg forgiveness.

He'd ruined everything. Her reputation. Her standing in the community. Watching her give that speech, he'd known then that the two of them were over. She'd been brimming with enthusiasm and resolve, convinced she wouldn't take no for an answer. Until she'd had to face her father. It was unrealistic to think she could change the patterns of a lifetime overnight. He had some nerve expecting her to change a damn thing.

"Thanks for letting me speak," he said, turning to Shea and catching another glimpse of Melanie, her gaze focused on her tightly clasped hands.

"Thank *you,*" Shea said. "I can't imagine a more convincing testimonial."

"Melanie, did you know?" Someone in the audience shouted over Shea. "Did you go with him knowing he's an ex-con?"

"No, she didn't," Lucas said, surveying the crowd, searching for the speaker. Not that he gave a shit who it was. "My past wasn't relevant until now."

Not many people agreed with him, judging by their hostile expressions. And Melanie… She didn't so much as make a sound. "What did you do, Sloan?" The guy who owned the filling station was standing in the back. "What'd they lock you up for?"

"Again, that's irrelevant," Lucas said, and Shea jumped in.

"Okay, we're done. We vote tomorrow."

Everyone started grumbling at once. They obviously hadn't had enough drama for one night. Lucas was already headed for the door. Shea was nuts for delaying the inevitable. She had to know how the vote would go. Why not just get it over with? It would take only a minute. He doubted he'd stick around until tomorrow.

He stopped when he got to the door. Much as he wanted to get out before people cornered him with nosy questions, he had to check on Melanie. Maybe she'd surprise him. Say the hell with everybody and follow him to his truck. His last shred of hope died the second he saw her.

She hadn't moved. The rest of the board members were

on their feet. She sat very still, her stunned gaze locked on her father. Lucas doubted she even knew he'd left.

Man, he needed a drink. It sucked that the Watering Hole was pretty much his only option.

Luckily, the place was dead. A couple of cowboys sat at a table. A few more were shooting pool in the back. Everyone looked over when he walked in, then turned away.

He found a spot at the end of the old mahogany bar and ordered from the dark-haired bartender. She gave him a friendly smile. He hadn't gotten many of those today. He took his first burning gulp of whiskey, then ordered another. The door opened, but he couldn't bring himself to see who might be looking for him.

"Nikki, he doesn't need a tab." It sounded like Sadie, so he glanced up. "Your drinks are on me," the older woman said, as she slipped behind the bar. "Just don't go getting stupid drunk."

"Nope." He drained the glass, then reached in his pocket for money. "I'm having two and that's it."

The door opened again, and in spite of himself he looked. Yep, it was a board member.

"Unless you're voting yes, get the hell out of here," Sadie said, glaring at the man, her big fist coming down hard on the scarred wood. "So help me God, I mean it, Abe."

Lucas smiled, though he'd almost jumped off the stool at the loud boom. Good thing she was on his side.

"You," she said, turning to him, "are a brave man. I respect what you did today. Don't be a coward now when it really counts." She gave him a meaningful stare. He just wasn't sure what it meant. Her eyes narrowed. "You know what I'm getting at. You just proved you know when something's worth fighting for." She lowered her voice. "But you still have work to do. That girl needs you."

Lucas had no idea how well Sadie knew Melanie. His guess was not very well or she'd understand that above everything, Melanie needed validation from her parents and the community. She didn't need a damn thing from Lucas.

With his outburst, he'd pushed her into an untenable situation. His lie may have helped, but not by much. It felt like hell. Funny how he'd known Peggy half his life and Melanie only ten days, but the pain he was feeling right now was so much worse. He hadn't even realized how much he'd fallen for her until he'd lost her.

Guess his luck hadn't changed that much. He was a fool for thinking he might have a real chance with a woman like Melanie. She deserved so much better.

While Sadie was busy pouring a drink, he finished his second whiskey, tucked some money under the glass and, tail between his legs, headed for the door.

MELANIE PUSHED ASIDE her untouched dinner, ignored the stack of papers she should've been grading and stared at her phone. Lucas wasn't going to call. Why should he? What would he want with a coward like her?

She supposed she could call him. But did she really want to talk to him? She could only imagine the disappointment in his voice, and that was bad enough.

Her phone beeped. She scrambled for it, sending papers flying off her kitchen table, her heart thumping wildly.

It was David.

She thought briefly about letting him go to voice mail. And then, like the good obedient girl she'd been most of her life, she answered.

"I hope I'm not disturbing you," he said, his voice confident with victory.

"I'm tired. I was finishing up some papers so I could go to sleep early." That was half-true. She wouldn't sleep. Every time she closed her eyes, she could still see the stunned looks of the board members and the townsfolk, the disapproval on her father's face, and she hated herself for being so weak.

"You're doing the right thing, Melanie," he said gently.

"Which is?"

He hesitated. "I hope you've gotten that man and his ridiculous program out of your system. You have too much at stake with your Safe Haven project, and now that everyone knows about his criminal record…well, it would be difficult for me to protect you." He paused. "As a teacher, you're a role model whether you want to be or not. But it's not too late. We can put this all behind us."

Melanie wasn't sure whether to laugh or cry. The contrast between David and Lucas had never been more obvious. Lucas might be an ex-con, but he was a man of principle. Whereas the principal was not even a man. "Good night, David."

Before he had a chance to respond, she'd disconnected and turned off her cell. But she couldn't shut off his words. He'd called her a role model, and she supposed that was true. She had students who might think she was old-fashioned, but they did, for the most part, look up to her. At Safe Haven she was valued not just for showing up but for taking responsibility for her extracurricular programs, instigating innovative techniques, not to mention the board position she would be resigning soon. And at church? She was her mother's daughter, her father's assistant, her community's touchstone and all-around gofer.

Before she turned off her laptop, she checked one final email. It was her father's Sunday sermon. Right on time. As if the evening hadn't even happened. When she saw the subject, she had to laugh. *Forgiveness.*

Perfect.

LUCAS LAY BACK in the bed of his truck, tucked into his old sleeping bag, staring up at the stars. He'd left the Sundance after thanking Rachel for her hospitality and leaving $400 on the nightstand.

No one at the Sundance had said anything about the fiasco at the meeting, but that was because they were good folks who didn't need the headache of him staying with their female guests. Before the night was over, he'd be the scandal of the year around here.

The air was damn chilly, and he'd thought about driving to Kalispell. Not for the motel bed—for the distance. But no matter how he sliced it, he couldn't leave just yet. He owed Melanie an apology, and not one he could send via text or even a phone call.

God, he could kick himself all the way back to Wyoming, but it wouldn't change the fact that he'd lost it tonight, and it had cost someone who mattered. For a year he'd tried so hard to keep things light, keep himself separate, and here he was smack in the middle of a small-town drama as the villain.

What the hell was he doing traveling the West to save wild horses? He couldn't even remember what it felt like to feel at home. Well, outside of Melanie's arms, at least, and he doubted he'd be welcomed there again.

Going to his ranch had been a wake-up call. Being a giant dope, he'd actually imagined the place cleaned up again. With special attention paid to the kitchen and the bedroom. He'd pictured the two of them away from the madness of this stifling town, spending their nights together. He'd be exhausted until he hired some help. She'd be busy, and not just cooking or cleaning or any of that stuff. The minute she got there, she'd have found out about the animal shelter, the local schools and the 4-H club. She wouldn't have the heart to say no to any of them, and he'd never say no to her.

He closed his eyes, banishing the useless daydreams. But not the idea of taking back his ranch. He'd be bound to run into Jessup, but the man didn't have the power to hurt him anymore. Truth was, if he tried something low like injuring the livestock, Lucas would stop him. Prison hadn't taken away the most important part of him. But he'd stop Jessup by using the law and not his fists.

Going back to face the biggest disappointment in his life, save the one he'd caused here, was the next step for him. Even without Melanie by his side, he needed to go home. Restake his claim. But first he had to face her tomorrow. See exactly what he'd lost.

SOMEHOW, MELANIE HAD managed to avoid David all morning, but there was no getting around him at the vote. He was in the same seat, and there was her father, right next to him. The town hall was at capacity, but this time there were friends and supporters. Rachel and Matt, Sadie, Nikki and Trace. Some of the teachers from the school. And wouldn't you know it, somehow Gertrude had finagled the Lemon sisters into getting her to the hall.

Mercifully, Shea refrained from reading the minutes of last night's meeting, and already the grumbling was starting.

Jesse stood up. "Look, when we opened the doors to the community, it wasn't so you could take over. You want to vote on Safe Haven policy, you can sign up to volunteer. But if anyone starts any trouble tonight, we're going to lock all of you outside."

That went over like a brick through a window, but Shea glared at the dissenters, refusing to move forward. Melanie took one more look at David, at her father. And she stood up, asking to make a statement.

It got quiet, and she just inhaled, let her breath take away her fears and began. "Last night a valued member of our town pointed out to me that I'm not just a volunteer at Safe Haven. I have responsibilities in this community. He called me a role model. I thought a lot about that. He was right. I *am* a role model. Which made me wonder what kind of message I'm giving my students, the people who attend my church, who I meet in the market and on the street. I realized pretty quickly that I haven't been a very good example. I've done chores, I've taught the curriculum, I've mucked the stables and more. But that's not all I am. Well, not all I want to be.

"Last night I watched a man stand up in a new town and bare his painful past to a group of people who'd called him scum. He carried himself with dignity, but not for his own gain. To help with rehabilitation in a system that's overcrowded and desperate for answers. He left his own ranch to be on the road to save wild horses, to give animal sanctuaries a chance to give their charges a real future.

"Lucas Sloan humbled me, and I would hope he's touched all of you, too. I didn't stand up for him last night, and that's my own failing. One I'm correcting now. I am not just a daughter, a teacher, a volunteer. I'm more than that. I have been there in one way or another for many of you in this room. And when I tell you that I've seen the power of this program to help horses, men and society, I expect you to listen. To respect me enough to know that I have proven myself to be honorable.

"Last night I read my father's next sermon. It's going to be on forgiveness. This Sunday he'll be telling you himself that forgiveness without action is meaningless." She started to take her seat but stopped. "You know, I've spent most of my life cowed by fear that I'd disappoint my parents or you people. It never once occurred to me that you would all disappoint me." She looked at the board members. "Be braver than I was last night. Don't let personal feelings get in the way of doing the right thing."

She inhaled sharply, as shocked as her father seemed

to be that she'd made such a speech and that she hadn't fumbled or fallen apart.

And when a few people started clapping, a lump formed in her throat, and then everyone but Earl stood up. David was the last to give in, but it was heartening to know her father had been the first.

Now she was trembling, and she couldn't wait to sit down. Except, there. In the back of the room, standing tall and staring straight at her with a look of wonder… Lucas. Her heart nearly beat out of her chest.

She nodded at him, and he nodded back, but that was all she could do, because Shea had quieted the room and called for the vote.

With a show of hands, the motion to participate in the Wild Horse Training Program carried unanimously. But that was only because Abe was getting the evil eye from Sadie.

The meeting adjourned, and she had to fight her way through a throng of people who wanted to say a good word. It was all she could do to be polite.

Finally, Lucas was there, right in front of her. "I thought you'd left."

Looking past her, he took her hand in his and headed for the door. They made it outside, but he kept on pulling her down the street, not stopping until they were hidden behind his truck.

She thought he might take her in his arms, but he didn't. She almost said something, but the way he looked at his feet, then slowly met her gaze stilled her.

"I couldn't go without telling you how sorry I was for last night."

"It was a shock," she said. "But it was also the bravest thing I've ever seen."

"I shouldn't have put you in that—"

She hushed him with a finger to his lips. "It's okay. I

know what you did and why, and I'm fine. I almost gave myself a coronary tonight," she said. "I didn't even have anything written down."

He laughed, and it felt as if all the achy places inside her were healing. "You were incredible."

"*We* were incredible."

"Yeah, I suppose we were. But that's not what I wanted to tell you." He pulled her into his arms, up against his strong, safe chest. She looked up into his eyes, waiting, feeling the quick steady beat of his heart.

"I'm going to be busy for a while after tonight. I have to get details worked out with you and Shea, then go to Denver for a sit-down. My work schedule needs to change. I'm going back to my ranch, honey. It's gonna be a long time before it's fit, but when it is, I'd like you to come see it."

"Why do I have to wait—?"

He smiled, then hugged her tighter, when already she could barely breathe. "Because," he said before lightly kissing her, "I'd like you to consider staying awhile. Like, say, a lifetime."

She finally caught the breath he'd stolen. "I think you skipped a step."

"Ah, you mean the part where I tell you I'm in love with you? That I can't imagine my life without you?"

It was her turn to smile. "Yeah. That part."

"I'm in love with you, Melanie. I got it bad."

"Well, that makes two of us." She wrapped her arms around his neck and kissed him back until they had to pull apart to breathe.

His expression was serious as he brushed her cheek with his fingers. "It won't be easy," he said. "We can see each other on weekends and holidays, but it'll take some time before we can truly be together, and then you'll just have me. I wasn't kidding about you thinking it through."

She leaned into Lucas. "A week ago I never could've

imagined that I'd ever walk away from Blackfoot Falls, from everything I've known. But I'd never dreamed of meeting a man like you, either. I'll think it through, give my parents time to get used to the idea of me living six hours away, but I already know what I want." Melanie smiled. "You're not the only one who's got it bad," she said before she kissed him.

* * * * *

Double Exposure

by Erin McCarthy...

Emma shifted on the seat of Kyle's car, hoping she wasn't smearing paint onto the upholstery. Why on earth had she volunteered to do this stupid group photo shoot? With the coworker she secretly craved, no less? The sooner she got this paint off and some clothes on, the sooner sanity would reappear.

"Can I take a shower at your place?" Maybe properly clothed she would be less aware of Kyle and her reaction to him. Because she could not, would not—ever—indulge herself with Kyle. Dating and sex made people emotional and irrational. It didn't mix with work.

"Of course you can." Kyle pulled out of the parking lot for the short trip to his place.

She caught sight of herself in the visor mirror. She looked worse than she'd thought. There was no way Kyle would ever come near her like this. Her hair was shot out in all directions, and her skin was emerald-green, with the whites of her eyes and her teeth gleaming in contrast. The napkins she'd used to cover herself tufted up from her chest. "I look like a frog eating barbecue!"

Kyle started laughing so hard he ended up coughing.

"It's not funny!" she protested.

Before they could debate that, he turned in to his building. Still chuckling, he ushered her toward the stairs. "What a day." He tossed his keys onto the table inside the entry of his apartment. "Bathroom's this way. Come on."

Emma followed, her eyes inevitably drawn to his tight butt. He was muscular in an athletic, natural way. Her fingers itched to squeeze all that muscle.

"I'm really good at keeping secrets, you know." Kyle turned, his eyes dark and unreadable.

She was suddenly aware of the sexual tension between them. They were mostly naked, standing inches apart. His mouth was so close....

"If anything happens here today, you can be sure it will never be mentioned at the office."

"What could happen?" She knew what he meant, but she needed to hear confirmation that he was equally attracted to her.

"This." Kyle closed the gap between them.

Emma didn't hesitate, but let her eyes shut as his mouth covered hers in a deep, tantalizing kiss.

Pick up DOUBLE EXPOSURE by Erin McCarthy, available wherever you buy Harlequin® Blaze® books.

HBEXP79808